The Outlaw Series

by **Kevin Boileau**

Illustrated by Ethan Claunch

also by
Kevin Boileau

Theory

Genuine Reciprocity and Group Authenticity
First Edition

Genuine Reciprocity and Group Authenticity:
The Social Ontology of Sartre & Foucault

The Algebra of History
(*with David A. Boileau*)

Essays on Phenomenology and the Self

Manifesto on Solidarity:
Ethics for a New World

Coming Soon

The Psychoanalytic Approach to Mediation

Game Theory, Mathematics, & Mediation

The Phenomenological Approach to Mediation

Literary

A Reason and A Season

The Patient

The Blue Pearl

Abject Poverty

99 Deceptions

The Separation

The Return

Coming Soon

3 Rivers

The Bishop...A Fisherman

Northside

Sexxxual Lies

Reproduction or translation of any part of this work beyond that
permitted by the United States Copyright Act without the permission
of the copyright owner is unlawful. Requests for permission or further
information should be addressed to:

EPIS Press
31 Fort Missoula Road, Suite 4
Missoula, MT 59804 USA
epispublishing1@gmail.com
www.episworldwide.com
www.episjournal.com
www.episeducation.com

Heart-of-Fire is an imprint of
EPIS Press

The Heart-of-Fire name and logo
are trademarks of EPIS Press

Printed in the United States of America
Library of Congress
1. Ontological Violence 2. Psychoanalysis
3. Phenomenology 4. Morality 5. Death
6. Title

Cover Design: Tia Hopkins
Cover Art & Illustrations: Ethan G Claunch
Author Photo: NTG
Author Seal: Adrian Balasa

ISBN 978-0-9899301-0-9

The Outlaw Series

Explorations in Ontological Violence

The Beginning

By Kevin Boileau
Illustrated by Ethan Claunch

We live in dark times, in which a navigation of the good life has become a shadowy cul-de-sac unless one opts for pre-ordained, formulaic roadways and directions. The architectonic of the possibilities of subjectivization operates in the netherworld of the unconscious, pushing and pulling, directing and sometimes commanding our performance.

And we disobey.

~~~

PREFACE

I realized that I had been part of the living dead, stepping through life in a mediocre way. I was so stuffed inside my head with moral conservatism that I could no longer feel. This was at the root of my own suffering. I had so safely ensconced myself in moral safety that I had become an automaton, pushed along by the logic of my bourgeois life and professional values.

Unfortunately this mediocrity had led to a giant gulf between my wife and me. She was slipping away but I did not know how to draw her back, given the atmosphere of toxic resentment in which I existed. My sin was unforgiveable. It was not so much that I had murdered someone. Rather, it was in the way that I did it. I had been coerced and for this reason it was not a free act. Thus my deeper sin was that I had committed an un-free act and this was antithetical to the coherence of my life as well as to the ideology that I had been spouting for decades. I was my non-self.

I went back to the bathroom and found a clean razor blade. I took off all my clothes and showered myself, enjoying the searing pain of the hot water that I allowed to scald my flesh. Then I sat down with a fresh, white towel at my feet, and I started cutting myself with the sharp blade. I wanted to cut open my chest, where my heart was. I wanted to carefully remove the chunks of skin that were situated between the sin-drenched outside world and the clean purity of my inner self. I wanted to lay open a doorway so that my inner cleanliness would spill out into the world I shared with others. I was willing to do this.

I took the blade in my hand and moved it close to my chest where my heart was. I held it against the skin and could feel the cold sharpness pressed against me, ready to split my soul. I held it for quite some time until I pulled the blade from my chest. In one, smooth, circular motion I brought the steel against the bicep of my left arm until blood oozed from my skin. I pressed harder and winced from the pain.

Watching the blood drip onto the white towel at my feet was hypnotic. I'd given myself a good cut so there was plenty of dark red liquid spilling onto the floor. Some if it landed on my feet, which felt odd because it was such a rare sensation. I was dripping onto myself. I felt ashamed, conscious of my fledgling attempt at destruction, at overcoming my own weakness. I became aware of my own consciousness about the shame and nervously looked at the clock by the mirror. Milena had been gone for over an hour but I figured that I still had some time left.

I had reduced myself to a man sitting naked in a bathroom cutting himself with a razor blade. My shame continued to bleed onto the towel as I tried to calculate how much time I had left before she came home. I reached the razor back up to my breast one, two—-three times—-before I gave up. Each time I brought the blade against my skin, next to my heart, I stopped. I used another towel to wipe the sweat out of my eyes. To top it off I was sexually excited. Perhaps it was the exhilaration I felt over seeing the blood spew out of me, the fact that I was a voyeur in my own life. I was excited.

I sat motionless, back in the trancelike state I had been in while Milena and I were talking in the kitchen earlier. The blood dripped and I sweated. The clock ticked. Then I heard the car in the garage. She was home. I jerked myself upright and quickly cleaned up my mess as I had many times before. I could easily explain the cut on my arm. It was the shame in my heart that was not so easily hidden.

I heard her downstairs. "I'm home," she announced. I hurried up and got a small bandage on my arm just as she rounded the corner into our bedroom. She had moved so fast up the stairs that she startled me in my semi-naked arousal. She averted her eyes but it was too late. We had both caught each other's privacy and she giggled a bit to lighten the sobriety of the moment.

Upon her urging I allowed her to look at my wound. She cleaned it up even better than I had, and re-bandaged it in her graceful and gentle way. I think she sensed that I needed her to ask me about the wound so she talked to me about it. I explained it off as an accident but I could tell that she was not entirely buying it. However, her attempt to inquire into my being and my state of mind, though, was a refreshing difference from her usual passivity. We spent the rest of the afternoon, and the evening, enjoying a few drinks and some friendship.

After dinner, I retreated to my new downstairs workspace. It was just the one light bulb and my workspace and the boxes of Rachel. I still figured that someone had to die. Milena's friendship with Lyken would end naturally.

~~~

One Saturday I took a break from the clinic and spent the day at my office. It was rainy and I could hear the steady dripping of water right outside my window. It made me think of the blood.

I had made a pot of coffee, and after I read the newspaper and shuffled through some papers, I lay down on my couch, pulled a blanket over myself, and closed my eyes. I listened to the splattering of the rain and formulated my plan.

I was going to do it. After weeks and months of solid reflection on the matter, I had firmly decided that he must die. I wasn't sure how I was going to make this happen. I did know that the world would be better off without him, especially the unfortunate individuals who got in his way. This is not to say that I knew precisely what he had been doing, but I'd had enough exposure to him to understand his nature.

He was a predator, weak in his family but so forcefully resentful in the social world that his pathology was dangerous and irrepressible. I felt responsible for him. He had come to me for therapeutic help and I fear that I had inadvertently exacerbated his condition. Knowing that I had killed someone myself—-albeit under coercive circumstances—-seemed to fuel his own rage and self-justification. He was dangerous but it was not as simple as turning him over to the authorities. Perhaps he could escape the clutches of the law while exposing me to prosecution. Even so, the matter was deeper than that.

I resented him. I despised him because he lived in a different moral universe than me, lacking the sorts of internal recriminations that I suffered. It was easy for me to characterize his pathology, of course, but this was a cheap victory and brought little comfort. The fact of the matter was that he did not beat up on himself like I did. It was true that when he first came to me for treatment he seemed paralyzed and crippled. Since then—-right around the time he had committed his first kill—-his overall situation had improved. This was near to the day he had discovered that it was I who killed the unfortunate man in the alley.

He was now vibrant and resolved, confident and cheerful, and lacked the kind of self-deprecation that I experienced every day. I was internally divided. He was not. Somehow he had managed to accept his aggressive propensities whereas I could not. Derivatively, it was so far impossible for me to accept his disposition when I had been his doctor. I am sure that his craving for blood had only deepened and strengthened.

How I would complete the purification, I didn't know, but I ruminated the possibilities all day as I sat in my office and listened to the rain splatter against the window. At one point I opened it, raising the large wooden frame with both my hands until the rain pelted me in my face. I held my cupped hands out to it and captured several handfuls. I cleansed my face with the water as I looked outside into the gray-black of the clouds and prayed for relief.

Afterwards, I closed the window snugly, dried myself off with a corner of a blanket, and sat at my desk in the dark, save for the narrow beam from the lamp that penetrated into my papers and into the book that I was reading. The phone rang and it was Milena offering to meet me for dinner (We did meet later and feasted on a warm meal of French onion soup, bagette, and a large salad, with crisp wine and a cup of hot coffee at the end.).

I could have him killed, I thought, or do the job myself. He was a tortured soul, I had concluded, and this allowed me the belief that his death would actually be a healing process for him. I quickly dismissed the notion of hiring someone to do the job for that would be too messy and careless. Besides, I knew that this was something I had to do myself.

I could stab him, shoot him, poison him, or run him over with a car. After brainstorming for several hours I decided that these were all too messy, and that the simplest way to complete his treatment would be to strangle him. I wouldn't hurt him too much. Rather, I would merely interfere with his ability to take in oxygen. That way he'd go fast and there wouldn't be much to clean up. I also considered whether I should stage a hold-up or a break-in and decided against these and similar plots. I'd keep things simple. I'd follow him, monitor his patterns, and when the time was right, do it. Those days my head was swimming with the realization that I would release him from the pain of his own consciousness. It seemed an act of completion and fulfillment. It would be a natural justice.

I cut myself in the office the day that it had rained so hard. I had a knife with me so I cut my thumb and squeezed the blood until it spilled onto the paper towels I had lined up on the floor. It spilled out of me in time with the pulsing of my heart. It was so pure, I noticed, the dark red droplets clinging to the towels as they held my gaze.

Memories of my first few years with Milena started jumping at me like excited puppies, indefatigable in their quest for connection. During those times she had approached me with an innocent purity I had never known, and even now she was my main connection to everything. Her original love for me was of the same quality as the youthful innocence Rachel had exemplified as she started her first stages of womanhood. It was like pure stillness. It was like dark-red blood. It was like the wind blowing near the cabin north of town. It was one of the last times I actually cut myself.

Midday, I called her. I felt her absence in my soul and all I wanted was for her to be next to me, my arms around her shoulders, and her breath in my ear. I'd love to be sitting with her at our rustic cabin north of the city, holding hands for hours as we watched the flames in our fireplace burn down to the dark blue, red-yellow-orange embers that followed.

With regard to my problem about Lyken, I'd take care of it with simplicity and then I'd be free. I could go on as before, ministering to the unwell and the confused, re-engaging with Milena, re-attaching myself to the stories I'd lived with my whole life. I'd strangle him. I'd block the wind from his lungs until he fell to his knees, until he collapsed. I continued circulating these ideas in my head until the blood soaked completely through the paper towels, staining the floor.

During the following week I made several trips to the public library, looking at books about the anatomy of breathing, gaining great insight into the mechanics of the cardio-vascular system of human beings. I also poured over many detective stories and perused many accounts of strangulation, both accidental and otherwise. This was my way. I would always educate myself about some topic, an issue, or a problem; learn as much as I could about it. Then I'd make a plan and execute it. Today was no different. I would be very careful.

One night when Milena was out with friends, I stayed late at the office, then headed toward one of the public cemeteries in the city. It was adjacent to the large park where I'd seen Lyken sitting on the bench with Milena. I shuddered, recalling the image of the two of them talking, knowing that they had been in a support group together.

I went to the cemetery but the iron gates were locked. I walked the perimeter, guiding myself by the moonlight. It was crisp out. It was not too cold, just enough to keep me alert. A dog barked and I strained to see. Cars rushed by down on the street but up here walking along the cemetery fence I was alone. Quite by luck I found an imperfection in the fence where I could press myself between the bars.

After I got inside I looked about, guiding myself by the moon. Off in the distance all I could see was a mass of shadows. Closer to me I could make out the headstones. I adjusted my scarf to keep warm and I set out on foot across the well-groomed blades of grass that separated the dead from each other.

A long time ago I used to hang out in a cemetery with a girl I knew. She was always keen on taking pictures there. She claimed that she could see the spirit world and hoped it would show up on her film. In my own recollection none of that ever happened but there was something so invigorating about being amongst the decaying flesh that we always ended up in sexual congress. I felt that now as I remembered the way she was able to throw off her clothes without a care in the world.

She—-and I always forget her name—-was wild and free, and I think that I resented her for it. I was always so busy figuring out what I should do that I lost sight of what I wanted to do. I lived out of obligation. She just lived. I think this is why we parted company. As I made my way slowly between the headstones, I was thinking about the way she had taken the pictures, getting just the right kind of light, approaching the necropolis as if she already belonged there.

But now I was here alone, trespassing, thinking about my own inevitable death, creeping among the headstones with a determined attitude. The girl I used to meet at the cemetery had moved to Europe within months after we first met so I never got to know her that well. But I always resented her way, much like I resented Lyken, much like I had mixed feelings about Milena's positive transformations.

I had no specific objective here other than to be with the dead. No one else was around. It was just the shadows, which allowed me access to my feelings and thoughts about my recent decision. Someone had to die and it was up to me to take care of it. I was a midwife.

I heard a siren in the distance and jerked my head up to see what was going on. It was too far away, however, and the trees at the edge of the graveyard blocked my vision. I kept walking deeper into the cemetery, thinking about the girl with the camera, musing about Lyken and my motivations.

A slight wind came up so I buttoned my jacket more tightly. I heard a sound to my left so I stopped walking, my heart racing. It was really dark so I couldn't see anything, but I no longer felt alone. I felt connected. I wasn't afraid, and I could see in my mind's eye the girl taking my pictures in the graveyard years ago, in a different town. My head was swimming with thoughts about the guy I killed, my plans to move Lyken into the netherworld, my wife. I could hear Dr. Black's voice in my ear: "You seem angry," he said.

Had I taken my knife with me I would have contemplated cutting myself, spilling my life onto the ground with the dead, mixing with them. Instead I was focused on my arousal, thinking back to the girl who had commanded my erotic attention in the graveyard years ago. I sat amongst the headstones for quite some time, feeling the wind pick up and tear through me like a sharp blade. I didn't move. I let my thoughts race through my mind and then out again.

I had an idea. He always stayed late at the clinic on Friday nights so he could finish his work. That's when I'd make my move. It'd be dark and no one would know. Just like it was dark here in the cemetery it would be dark down in the ghetto, near the clinic. I was now firmly committed to the act. I had to put latex gloves on the list.

I left the cemetery invigorated and resolved, feeling virile and young. I was feeling powerful. I almost had a joyful feeling as I angled myself through the imperfection in the fence that separated the living from the dead. Everything felt open. The streets and the buildings, lit up with neon, and did not appear to close in on me. My head was high and my posture erect. I was a confident man heading toward a confident life. As I drove away from the graveyard, I looked back at the dark. I could almost see the girl snapping my picture and Dr. Black recording it all.

When I got home I waited for Milena to arrive. I was actually excited to see her, so I sat at the small writing desk in the entryway and sorted through some correspondence. My father had written me, explaining how sad he was that my mother had passed. His handwriting was hard to read but I was able to see that there wasn't much left for him. He hadn't gathered many rosebuds during his life and the most important one was now only a memory.

from The Patient (published 2011) by Kevin Boileau

ONE:
HAYES
CREEK

I bought the gun when I left the city. I left because I hated their ways. Then I bought the gun and headed for outlaw territory. If they came after me, I knew I'd use it. I'd just point and fire like the expert had shown me.

I swung the old Ford truck out of my Dad's driveway in the early morning, going south to the outlaw country. I was set to pick up a 30.06 from a gun dealer on the way out of town, with enough ammunition for the summer. He'd have my fall supply ready for me when I came back through, he said. I noticed he didn't look up—this was part of the western respect I'd craved. This was part of the reason I left the city.

I couldn't make it in Bourgeois-ville. This is why I left. The moral prescription was outside of my predilection and outside my natural talent. When I figured this out I realized I had no choice except for the one I'd made. I looked at the pistol on the old faded red vinyl seat and the rifle on the rack just above the rear window.

I smiled.

-2-

I got an apartment and a job at the local convenience store. They fired me two weeks later, saying the "till was off" but I quickly got hired at the Wal-Mart. For a while I felt a sense of freedom until I realized my supervisor was going to pick at me until he figured he could control me.

"Did you do the inventory?"

"Bathroom check?"

"What about special orders?"

It wasn't what he said that bothered me. Instead, it was the timing and the tone, so one day I stole money out of the register, threatened him, and quit. That's when I got the guns and headed south into the old cowboy country with my Ford.

Four hours south I got to Hayes Creek and naturally stopped at the Hayes Creek Diner.

-3-

"Coffee?" she asked. I looked up affirmatively like the gun dealer had and got a pretty little smile in return. A week later I took her virtue in the car, and headed down to Red Rock Lake for the weekend. She told me later that she thought I'd never come back, even though I left some of my books for her at the diner.

It was in the morning when I left and the blue skies and clean mountains afforded me solace—until I saw the lawman's red light in my rearview.

It was an ugly encounter. I had tried to be polite but something about my out of state plates must have pissed him off because he became belligerent and started picking at me for the guns.

Something inside me snapped. All the years working for the Establishment: being constrained in my actions; being pinned even in my consciousness.

After the wolf came to me in my dream everything changed. I became angry toward all oppressors, which unleashed even more rage. I read. I ate differently. And then the encounter with the Sheriff happened. Afterword, I could see the blood trickle out from behind his left ear as he lay in the sagebrush on the side.

I picked up the spent cartridges and put them in my pocket. Then I headed south into the Red Rock where I camped for two nights under the big sky.

~~~

After the campfire died down and it quieted, I fell into sleep. That's when the wolf came to me.

But this time he brought the eagle. I kept trying to get through the sliver in the rock. I'd climbed so far to even see the precipice with the eyelet, let alone understand that I could choose to walk through. As the night passed the opening grew larger and I climbed toward it. There, the eagle met me. It pulled me up the canyon wall to the eyelet: clutched at me until we became one and entered the eyelet together.

I fell back to sleep until I heard the helicopter and saw the law enforcement officers. They were looking for the person "of interest" who might know something about the murdered deputy. They got to me just as dawn broke. The campfire was still smoking so I put wood on it and offered them coffee. It got lighter in the East as the sun rose.

"Do you know anything about it?" they asked.

The wolf and the eagle sat at the top of the rock precipice, pointing to the eyelet—and I could feel strong blood coursing to my hand.

There were three of them, the main sheriff and two deputies, and as the conversation progressed, I could see that they suspected me. They wanted to know about my guns. After I filled their coffee cups and we talked, I could see that I had a choice to make. I could either let them arrest me, take me to jail, and perhaps kill me—or I could do what I'd always wanted: This was to act in accord with my nature, which I'd been holding back on for my whole life, in the city.

I decided on the latter, and after gaining their trust, I offered to show them my gun so they could see if it had been fired recently. While I still had them in my trust, I shot all three, quickly, one by one. Then I buried the bodies in the morning sun and drove south into the wilderness.

Never had I felt so alive.

After I buried the bodies and put sagebrush on the squad cars I left. The future no longer mattered anymore. It was only my present that was important. Never had I felt so free.

-4-

When I came back after two months, I drove into town, to the diner with the woman who thought she was my girlfriend.

She saw me sitting in the rear booth and smiled. I could see she was excited and hopeful, like she'd won a wager with the one of the voices inside her head. She almost curtsied as she poured the dark brown liquid into my cup. "Missed you," she said. I smiled, which gave her the message that I had missed her too.

It was busy so we made plans for later. After I had my way with her that evening, I convinced her to rob the diner—and to steal her roommate's rare paintings. She met me in the morning with everything I asked from her, and we drove off.

I knew it wouldn't be long before smarter law enforcement showed up so we drove clear across the state and north to a town called "Wheatbrush." There we got a cheap room on the outskirts of town. I made her get a job.

Meanwhile, I stashed the paintings and half the money in a shed and then proceeded to spend my time thinking up my next plan. I was far away from my former city life and content with that decision.

-5-

After I drove back to the gun dealer for the rest of my fall ammunition, I went back to the little town in the northeastern part of the state where the girl was working hard for us. I treated her just fine as we passed the fall frolicking but when the snow came I became restless.

It wouldn't be long until the law caught up to me here, so I started thinking we'd move on again. I'd already shot a man out on the outskirts of a nearby town—got his money and a wire transfer for more, so I figured eventually someone would start poking around.

Just after Thanksgiving I guess someone from the Red Rock Lake area called a sheriff, who put an APB out for me, and eventually it got to the north side of the state.

It was the way he looked up at me, violating the code not to stare at others in the face that told me he suspected me. We—the diner girl and I—were finishing our dinner at the local steak-n-potato and I could sense him looking. Then I saw him doing so, one eye at his plate, the other half-cocked toward me.

By noon the next day we were gone with the paintings, the stolen money, and everything else I could take. Late that day, I beat a gas station attendant along the northern route and got his money and gun, too. A television was on with our pictures and I didn't wish her any harm, so I put her on a bus back to Red Rock with a purse full of money. She cried but I made her go, then I stole a truck and headed toward the North Country. Once I got across the border I'd be safe for a while. I'd hole up until I could make a new plan and move to a new state and a new life.

I was between the old and the new, exploring what felt most sublime about my nature—and most lost. Yet, I smiled as I crossed. They never found me and I never got caught.

TWO:
THE WOLF
PACK

He read in the paper that they'd shot the wolf. He read that they thought this might subdue the wolf pack's propensity to kill sheep and other livestock. So they killed the wolf, one of nine, and the pack continued its ways, picking off a sheep here and there but neither increasing nor decreasing its tempo.

The ranchers claimed that the wolf was evil and ought to be eradicated. They said the wolf intended its "wrongful kills." So after a town hall meeting with the sheriff they decided to get a band of shooters together to eradicate the pack. Their intention was the genocide of the gray wolf out beyond the outskirts of town, at the edge of the county line.

That's when I spent the day cleaning my guns: the 30-30, the 30.06, the .45, and others. I listened to my Sears-bought, police-band radio to see when the hunt would occur. Then I checked my work schedule at the Big-Box Store.

I spent the next several days cleaning the guns, monitoring the police radio to make sure there were no changes to the marauder's schedule; dropped things at work; didn't listen to my boss, which pissed him off. And the guns got cleaner. On the way out of town I grabbed the 12-gauge and looked for the band of killers.

It was a dark and rainy day when they went out there; twenty of them with high-powered rifles to annihilate the eight. I'd spent my whole life living by the white man's rules—our rules—but I had little to show for it other than a pocket of principles and a dam about to bust in my head.

I was dressed like them, jeans and boots, flannel shirt and jacket, with a rain overcoat, my old faded-blue Chevy truck inching its way past the quarry. Gas gauge on half, truck still pushing out a strong heat, wipers pushing away the rain like tears. I had one on the rack; three on the seat. Then I saw them—like modern day elephant hunters.

They were in a caravan heading up the ridge to a trailhead. I veered away from their smoke and metal to a different road and a different trail. They were headed to Wolf Ridge and I'd cut them off in two hours before they could do what they intended.

I took the turn-off to Sunny Creek Road while they proceeded upward on Devil's Gate highway.

It became colder.

The barrels of all my guns were extensions of my hands and fingers there, the truck, and me, operating in unison as one being.

A slim arrow of sunshine bore through the cloud wall and the rainy film, lighting the way, late morning. The Indian paintbrush stood as mini-sentries, the dirt road caked with moisture.

Past the Last-Drink Saloon I made the turn and headed up to the cut-off point. I knew I'd probably lose the Big-Box job. Maybe I'd go to jail. Maybe I'd die. But it would be in a heroic moment of authenticity, finally standing in the lights instead of the shadows.

I briefly turned the dial to Cowboy Land Radio, my favorite

country music station since I graduated and entered the job market.

I had pictures of the Gray wolves strewn about the cab and the floor of my truck and in between songs I looked at them with reverence.

I hit a bump in the road, which knocked the radio out and a blast of water cascaded across my windshield.

I saw a lone wolf on the ridge. The killers were driving there. It was regal, still, standing and looking in the light misty rain. Then he was gone—the pack must be nearby, I thought, and focused my grip harder on the steering wheel.

After several more miles of bumps, rain splashes, and daydreams of lost opportunities, I pulled the truck off the road, grabbed the rifles, and headed through a well-covered ravine that would bring me just above the route of the wolf posse, on a ridge. I scurried up there quickly, and assembled my equipment on a rock ledge under a pine tree that shielded me from the rain.

I could hear them driving up underneath before I saw. I could sense the murderous spirit in the air as I grabbed the 30-06 with the scope. Then I watched them all get out, three or four from each of the handful of trucks, and assemble at the trailhead just below – boots, flannel, rain jackets. The trucks stood there in a circle, the men a mass of rifles.

I could hear the rain pelting down now as the men walked in single file up the trail, gradually quieting their voices as they each ratified the solemn mission before them. Yet, it didn't appear solemn. For some, there was sarcasm; others, sport. Still others, perverted, Stoic-moral duty. None of them mentioned how the humans had invaded the space and territory of the wolves.

I paused for just a moment to collect my thoughts and review my proposed course of action. If I did nothing these men would most surely destroy a beautiful wolf pack. My choice was clear. Therefore, I positioned myself carefully between two slabs of granite, waiting. I'd be able to pick off nearly half of them before they figured out what was happening. The rest I'd deal with as needed.

It was a blood bath. I waited until the nine or so were in plain view and picked them off with two rifles. As the smoke cleared amidst a clamor of voices, blood everywhere, the most sensible one said, "Over there. He's over there." "He's trapped," another added. With half of them attending to the two or three that were dying from gunshot, the others advanced carefully.

After it was all over, it was said that I'd killed them all. When they locked me up, they said I was a murderer. But after the trial was over and they sent me to the big House, everything changed. I strangled a guard and knifed a fellow inmate with a wood shank I'd carved. Then I escaped from the desolate walls, stole a car, and went to No-Man's Land, south of the Red Rock Lake. I never came back and they never found me.

More importantly, this changed the way I interfaced with the rest of society. As the years passed, I drifted from one town to another, first one city and then next, taking day labor and odd jobs to pay the rent.

I'd heard that family from the nine I'd shot had put a bounty on me, so I prepared for that. My former normal state of resentment became paranoia, but that gave way to a feeling of power and freedom. Since I lost my job, my community, friends, and everything else, and because I figured the law would eventually catch up with me, I no longer had the burden of considering governmental rules; I just did what I wanted and I tried to right the wrongs I saw. I was a dead, righteous man walking.

The man I saw shaking his petite wife I punched in the face so many times was a bloody pulp.

The perturbed driver of the luxury car fumed at the gouges I caused with my key.

The man who kicked his dog was a messy pile of blood, broken ribs, and an apology.

It became a constant for me, righting these wrongs, operating with my own code, subject only to my sense of balance and degree, punishing severely the stronger who hurt the weaker.

One day in a diner, I could hear a couple fighting in the rear booth so I sauntered inconspicuously to the other side of the counter so I could hear better. They were fighting about his jealousy and he was getting the better of her. Then I heard a quiet muffled grimace from her, which must have been from him pinching the blood out of her arm.

I sipped my coffee patiently while he continued to punish her. A few minutes later I followed him into the men's room. After he pissed, I took out the "punisher," as I called it and smacked him three times, once in the kidneys, once in the shoulder, and once in the face as he turned toward me. By then, he had slumped to the floor, all 250 pounds of him, the fat-ass, coward-bitch.

Then I kicked him hard in the ribs until I heard them crack, and spoke with a low, controlled voice: If you ever touch her again I'll kill you. I'll come and find you and hurt you slowly until you die. Then I will find your family and kill them one by one. Do you understand, you mother-fucking bitch?

He didn't say anything—the blood was oozing out of his

mouth and he was groaning but I knew he could hear me—
so I kicked him again. You rotten little sonofabitch.

I thought of the wolves that had been slaughtered.

THREE:
THE
BOOKKEEPER

I was the eldest brother, and had taken a job as a bookkeeper before I was even out of high school so that my younger brothers could have a better life. I didn't actually get my diploma because I needed to work during the day and this caused my expulsion.

Unfortunately, my teenage girlfriend had latched on to me, and by the time I was twenty-three we had two children, and a couple more later. By that time my brothers were out of the house and in college out of state. I received Christmas cards from them, usually the day before the holidays started with the kids and the wife. I'd usually work the Eve of it.

I dressed like the laborer that I was, although because it was an office job, I existed at the penumbra of the white-collar professional, though marginalized because of my lack of formal training. I had few credentials though I was well thought of for my diligence and circumspection.

My wife and I faced challenges daily, given our lack of funds and modest trajectories for the future. She was a pretty woman, not beautiful perhaps, but pretty, with the right curves that attracted attention. She worked as a hair stylist fulltime, for the money, so we had to hire younger babysitters to watch the kids while we were at work.

None of this was particularly fun or interesting, and within a few years, I realized that the situation I had gotten myself into was going to become a long path of drudgery, lifetime penury, and weariness.

"Can you pick up the kids?"

"I'm tired. I just want to sleep, okay"

~~~

Then from my boss: "I need you to stay late tonight."

Worse, he would say: "We are not making our numbers. We need to have a meeting about it."

~~~

From my family: "How are things going with the kids?" "Hope to see you over the holidays."

My back started hurting by the time I was thirty. Sex became an obligation that was regulated by her estrous cycle, to which I complied; otherwise the house became a mess. However, over the years I'd notice increasing lengths of her withdrawal. We had no money in our bank account and had severely high credit card debt.

We became roommates of sorts, parenting four children, with very little upward mobility in sight. Eventually the sex stopped and our interaction became family pizza early Friday nights just down the street.

I was out of shape, having accumulated a beer belly that was accentuated from the greasy, fatty, carbohydrate-rich foods that gave me momentary solace from my lot.

Being approached by the new girl at work in her twenties;

Hearing enough of my siblings' successes;

Becoming sick and tired of the grind of my job;

Worse: becoming constrained in the way I thought about the world; because my situation was so limited, the way I thought about things was inevitably lacking in imagination; because I was in a situation and I didn't know a way out:

I became edgy. The way words left my mouth transformed from the compassionate, pleasant delivery of my past and became edgy, brusque, and intolerant. My anxiety had increased, and correlatively, my impatience.

She and I became distant, performing our duties in perfunctory ways; I suspected she had another life elsewhere, given her propensity to "have lunch or go out with the girls." Her drinking increased. The babysitters got more time with the kids.

My boss pressured me for more time and a higher workload. I had no time to myself. And there was the tradeoff between my stress and the effects of drinking to curb it. Going to the Protestant church down the street became something I did for appearances, but I came to realize the degree of bullshit involved in it—cheating wives, beating husbands, stealing accountants, and generally nefarious behavior was "forgiven" just by attending.

-2-

One day, the owner, who was my boss, looked down his nose at me one too many times. He looked down his nose just over the glasses that rested below his eyes.

He'd been chastising me more than usual lately because profits had been down. The many years of his chipping away at my self-esteem had eroded most of the trust between us, and I no longer gave a shit about him. Coupled with my growing unrest about my home life, I had little repose that was free from the gnawing resentment that was percolating in me.

During lunch one day, I left without reason and ended up in a gun shop, plunking down a tattered credit card and what little cash I had to complete the transaction: The .38 felt just right in my hands, and after the wait period picked it up and hid it under the seat in the truck.

The following week I started going out to the edge of town where there were dirt piles, garbage, and a hodgepodge of old car parts and other odds and ends. I'd go out there with cheap caps and shot anything I could find: bottles, furniture, pictures—whatever.

I'd hold that pistol until my knuckles turned white, firing round after round of the cheap caps until they were gone; and I always felt better when I went back to work. After a couple of weeks of this, continued pressure by the owner, and a shit pile of suffering at home, I made my plan. I knew my wife had been "seeing" one of the neighbors when I was out at baseball or basketball practice with the kids. I hadn't actually seen them but I knew; I could feel it at the BBQs. And as far as my kids go, I had nothing against them. I didn't really know them because there was never enough time but my resentment went in other directions.

-3-

O nce I felt comfortable with the pistol I started wearing it in my belt sometimes, covered over only by a flannel shirt that hid the metal. It felt powerful in there, ready to wage war on anyone who triggered my all the frustration I had been carrying ever since high school.

I was at a dead-end, numbed and dying. I had no prospects and no way forward. I had been reduced to a beast of burden, and my life had been reduced to its lowest ebb except for the burning in my very core. That's when I made my plan.

Later that night, I went to the office to do some work after dinner. With metal pressing against my navel, I left the dinner table, kissing the kids, telling her that I'd be back later I wheeled the car out of the driveway. She'd been really keen on the exact time of my return, but I honestly couldn't say. "Much later," I said. "You can call me on the shop phone if you need me for anything," I added.

I knew he'd be there, reviewing inventory—looking at the books—making decisions about who to fire. Business was down, and he was feeling it. "You're here," he said, looking down his long beak at me, just over the top of his glasses. I felt the shame rising up in me but just as quickly gave it back to him. "I am," I pronounced. "I have to finish a few things before tomorrow." Then he ignored me and turned to his work.

I went to my office, a small little shithole of a room filled with an old desk, torn up hardwood, paneling, a couple of cheap paintings, and the file cabinets that were overflowing onto everything else. It was a total shithole with poor lighting except for the banker's lamp with a highly focused beam.

I put the gun in the drawer and sat down to a stack of work that had to be done by tomorrow or I knew I'd be in trouble—more criticism, more shaming—and I was done with that. The phone rang and she was there, reporting about the kids and wanting to know when I'd be back. I repeated that it would be much later and then she hung up. I knew where shed be going, but I didn't much care anymore. I was going to take care of things now.

~

I'd been working through the books for quite some time—maybe two hours—when I stopped by his office on the way to the bathroom.

"Aren't you done yet?"

I considered answering him but things were now beyond that. I went to the men's room to piss and then sat in his office for several minutes while he "talked" to me about business. It was during this conversation that I realized the gun was a prop. I also fully gestated a plan for my liberation.

Over the next several weeks, I shot the gun at the garbage heap—killing various objects—while I perfected my action steps.

Before the next winter, my boss died in a tragic car accident, my wife fell off a ladder and died, and my mother came to take care of the kids. I went back to school and lost fifty pounds. Nevertheless, I continued shooting caps wherever I could; since I was in a new city, I found a new garbage dump.

FOUR:
THE MEXICAN
LABORER

e Baffled
ODY FOUND ON SHORE
Serial Kil
Claims A
Killer on
SEASIDE KILLER
STRIKES AGAIN
Murdered
PANIC IN PARA

She would smile at them, often engaging them in polite conversation about their families. "How's business?" she would ask, motioning to the back of the old truck with items, as she called them, piled high.

"It's good," they would always say, not wishing to reveal weakness. The lead guy—the one who drove the old Ford—did most of the talking and the four or five he had with him would always follow his lead, taking care not to speak out of turn. It was a hierarchy.

Raul was his name, and he was only three generations removed from the seasonal farm pickers in California. With some native intelligence and a strong back he'd made it up the coast, had a bit of college, and then migrated into the "valley," somewhat removed from the "Island," as its inhabitants called it. This denomination enabled them to feel different, safe, and special.

He was still strong even though he was now in his 50s, with a great number of children, and his wife of many years. His years had taught him the value of judiciousness so he was always careful around these people on the island. He did not want trouble, for himself or any of the younger men he'd drive around to jobs.

The island was a true one, and had only been connected to the mainland with the help of the wealthy who afforded a roadway system that skirted its way across its northern shore. This was the only access point.

***

One day, on the weekend, one of Raul's men drove his old truck to the Island and sat at a park to watch people. He'd resented the way the blonde, white bitch had looked at him. He could tell that her friendliness had no truth in it and that she cared nothing for them.

P____ sat in his car at the park and watched the new moms parking their luxury SUVs, walking their children and pushing baby carriages, his hand tightening around the club, or on other days a knife or a pistol.

His own background had been very different.

Meanwhile, he continued to work for his boss, Raul, and to smile when the privileged women acknowledged his presence.

Smile and look down. Smile and look down. It would have been impolite to look at any of them in the eyes, for at least three reasons. First, he would have given away his desire for them and second he would have shown his resentment and hate. There was also the purely social aspect: it would have been a breach of etiquette.

P's home life was terrible: His wife was loving enough and beautiful; his kids were smart and talented. Even so, he had a hole in his heart from his own childhood. Things had happened that colored everything. But he grew, years passed, and he placed his cultural life, and everything went forward.

Eventually Raul assigned P various jobs, which meant that Raul sat in the office and P drove the truck. More often than not, that truck ended up at the Island, cleaning out what was left over from the weekend's estate sales, filled to the brim with what the usual pickers didn't want. All this junk ended up in the vacant lot next to Raul's place in the valley, protected by the chain-link.

After a few of these jobs, P's admixture of feelings accelerated into a cauldron of resentment, hate, and desire. There was something about his personality structure that precluded him from virtue except to the extent that it benefited him or his family. It was a "chip on his shoulder" someone had called it, and even though Raul could also see it, he wanted to give P a chance in life.

The jobs would usually go life this: Raul would get the call from one an estate sale manager and give the call to P. This would involve coordinating a handful of workers who would show up at a mostly-empty house to a) collect what hadn't already been picked over twice and b) to clean it out. On occasion, there were extra items elsewhere that had been bought and sold, and which had to be delivered to a buyer so P would do that too.

Inevitably, this brought P into contact with a number of strangers, including some of the estate sale managers who were mostly women. This also meant that he and some of the guys would pull up in front of house, manhandle various pieces of furniture into the truck, and then deliver them for cash money of which they received a small fee for their trouble. As P saw it, he and his guys did 90% of the work for 10% of the pay.

P would go home to his wife, complain in an even-handed way without her thinking that he was soft, and then after dinner retire to more beer and a few cigarettes. It went on this way for several months until P became bitter toward all of it, thereby alienating his children and his wife, and in some cases, his boss Raul. But he kept on at it, smiling at the rich white women on the Island, gathering the junk, and collecting a small pay that barely paid the bills.

If you had been there in the back yard with P, you would have noticed his hand clenching the beer cans with greater pressure, the blood pulsing in his temples with greater velocity, and his under-the-breath comments more excoriating.

Then a Wednesday came and he ended up on a job waiting for his men due to scheduling issues. He could tell that no one was home except for the arrogant women who had items left over from an estate sale the prior weekend. She'd waved to him from the front door, yelling for him to wait until she got off the phone.

There were items in the garage that she had for him—it had already been arranged through Raul but he had to wait and he was not in a mood for waiting. In addition, his men were late [unknown to him they had been called to another location to pick up some merchandise but he didn't yet know about it because he had accidentally turned off his phone].

So P paced the street in front of his truck. Then he walked into the driveway hoping to see the furniture he was supposed to haul away. Unfortunately he couldn't tell which of the pieces were for him so he walked up to the front door, eventually knocking, then banging on it.

One thing led to another and within five minutes the men still hadn't shown up, the matron of the house—perhaps 50 or so—hadn't gotten off the phone, and P had had enough.

He barged into her home: actually opened the front door and entered into the foyer. Didn't move when the phone rang. Didn't budge when she tried to shoo him out. By then she'd gotten off the phone and the men were on the way with the truck but it was too late.

She called him a name that was racially pejorative, which moved the situation beyond rudeness. It was a crucible, that moment in the foyer, and went he hit her-so hard-she slumped to the ground. You'd expect that maybe he would have stopped, seeing her down on the ground with a welt already starting on her forehead, but this was not the case.

Instead, he started kicking her in the ribs until he heard one or two crack then he paused. "Who the fuck do you think you are?"

He could have said more, easily, but didn't, and watched her watching him. She'd regained a bit of consciousness, enough for her to see him, and to gauge his next move. "I'm sorry," she forced out of her damaged rib case, but it was too late. He'd paused but only to strategize about how to hurt her further.

All this was recounted months later after the inquest, and the reports hesitated to go further, but suffice it to say that when he was done with her she was a bloody mess. She could barely speak, and after two minutes of watching her suffering, he regained his wits enough to realize that his team was on the way in one of the old trucks.

What had begun as out of control rage had quickly become calculating, strategic ratiocination. The truck loomed closer, oscillating beating the careening around corners and the slow passing of pretty women. The men leered, carefully, talking amongst themselves in ciphered words until they reached the turn off. At the same time P moved at the speed of light to clean up the blood and the shit in her pants. Her lifeless body didn't cooperate, however, and even someone as strong as him had to expend a great deal of effort to move her.

Five minutes later she was in a bag in the garage, covered in a carpet and a plastic wrap, and the foyer was clean. The one thing about him that people could agree on was that he was thorough in whatever he did. The bloody rags all went into another bag, and later he returned to do an even better job with ammonia. Meantime, the men arrived and they picked up the items in the garage that had been neatly marked: P wouldn't have had to wait except for the woman's insistence on it, but this had thereby become the capstone to her fate.

Raul made out pretty good on this job, and when the cops started poking around no one was the wiser. Since there was no body—it had been neatly arranged at the bottom of the river—there was technically no crime even though an investigation had ensued. Some time later divers found her body, which triggered a full on investigation, but since time of death couldn't pinpoint a day, the men were no suspects.

It was the sheer success of it that triggered P's blood lust, and it this event became the first of many. He was a quick learner and it only took him a couple more kills to become technically advanced and strategically aware.

Those around him noticed a change in his attitude, a sort of release that allowed him to be more at ease in social situations. With his newly found confidence he became a more attentive husband and a better father. The estate sale team enjoyed his joking around, and even Raul acknowledged the improvement.

However, there was a younger detective who started coming around, not so much on official business, but more so as part of the community. This did not deter P at all however and his crimes continued. After tiring of the affluent on the Island—which as all things become: boring—he looked for new hunting grounds.

Eventually he and Raul parted company, Raul moving to a more mixed, bourgeois neighborhood, P and his wife staying within their own ethnic group.

The local papers continued to write about a series of gruesome murders. It was someone who was very angry and full of rage.

P continued, cleverly arranging his misdeeds between his jobs so that he wouldn't stand out. At first his beautiful young wife knew nothing of it, but as time passed she sensed that something was wrong. Yet, she was afraid of him, especially after she saw what he did to the neighbor's cat.

P got his own truck and a couple of workers so he could compete with Raul, but this was unrealistic. His surly attitude and his commitment to principle kept him locked into bottom of the barrel jobs and a less than satisfactory income. The five kids didn't help, and neither did his wife's weight gain. Since he was devout he'd never consider cheating on her, but this actually added to the combustibility of his situation.

Investigators came and went throughout the city where the serial killer had rent his rage, including the two incidents on the Island where P occasionally took a job. P's behavior went through a number of revolutions, which included hunting in new areas, and experimenting with more sadistic forms of torture, including the toolbox and other paraphernalia. He got away with it because the jobs explained his whereabouts, the work his tools.

The newspaper recounted a certain level of detail of the crimes, but not enough to incite reaction. Then, when the whole matter was at its height everything stopped. The estate sale clean outs continued but the killings stopped. P's son H had just turned 14 this particular summer that the killings stopped, and the both of them started spending a lot more time together.

To all appearances he was just an ordinary boy, perhaps a little angry and mean but he seemed normal. P's wife was glad that her husband started taking their son on jobs—she figured it would keep him out of trouble. And in a certain way it did.

They'd drive together to the estate sale clean ups and within a few months the boy was not only driving, but he was learning how to run people off the road without getting caught; bullying people at the malls in a subtle way; preparing for more: They would go the hardware stores to shop for various goods, which included duct tape, rope, and various tools. Although the boy wasn't certain what they would be doing with them, he enjoyed spending the time with his father away from his siblings.

This went on until the killings began again in the fall. The investigators said that the profile had changed. Raul prospered.

FIVE: THE BUREAUCRATIC LAWYER

"**A** new case came in last night, Dyme," the senior lawyer said to his junior lawyer. "I know, I saw it come in on the fax machine. I was working in the library."

"You'll take care of it?" "Of course."

I put the coffee cup down on my mahogany desk and opened the file. It looked interesting: there was the accuser and the accused, some evidence, contradictory stories. It was my job to push the case through the system so that everyone could move on.

I'd gotten so good at it that I had grown fat in my complacence and dogmatic in my approach. Everything was routinized: My white shirts, the silk ties, pants with a short cuff, gas for the car—everything, and it had been going on for years until my waistline had gained 5 or 6 inches from when I had entered law school.

I read the case; it was about a couple from the Valley who were trying to split up. There had been accusations of bad behavior by both, innocent victims involved, and bureaucratic issues.

I put the file down, sipped the coffee, and then wandered down the hall. A few moments later there was a resounding smack on the wall from where I'd landed the palm of my hand where the cyst was—I had to do this every time the cyst re-grew itself from the last time.

I had other eccentricities as well, like peeing outside in the backyard, letting others taste food first, and cutting myself every time I became anxious. There were more violent acts, which were becoming more violent through time.

Striking motions were pleasing, like swatting the kitchen utensils at the flies. Cutting into the vegetables; stomping dirty shoes on the floor; pulling weeds; anything that involved the application of force. This started in kindergarten, followed to grade school and high school; then it migrated into college and beyond. Demanding that the furniture of the world yield to me felt like my right and privilege, drawing the blood of anyone who got in my way.

Why should accede my power to the weak? Why should I cow-tow to someone else's sense of propriety? Fit myself in to a program and a format that someone else had created, especially when I had never even been introduced to the architects?

I shot, I spit, I cut.

I pressed, I pushed, I forced.

And I continued my studies, which earned me a credit: the assumption that I was a member of the "Right and the Good." This, in turn, motivated a benefit of the doubt toward me which included a benign Gaze when, in fact, all I could think about was the application of force and the destruction of what had been established. This was not a naïve view of freedom; in contrast, it was just a personal aesthetic standpoint on the application of force.

Frequently, I would tear up paper into tiny bits before throwing them into the garbage, sometimes into a toilet at work. Sometimes, I would pull pens apart into their little pieces—the cartridge, the clicker, the spring, etc.—until they were completely annihilated, then they were off to the wastebasket.

No one knew of my propensities except for those closest to me, and while they openly chocked it up to nerves or frustration, they secretly knew better. They just didn't say anything. In exchange, I toed the mark at church and in school, performing in accord with expectations of decency and accomplishment. This hallmark allowed me my demand for force: my only scripture was to regulate its presence and degree.

This led to the law diploma and the bar license, a state-sanctioned approval of my demand for force! A laudatory conscription of my need for destruction! It was a true way to make invisible within the visible.

Thus, my life was productive and familiar, a closure that avoided any sort of critical self-reflection, which suited me just fine. I figured that as long as I was successful in what I was doing, I could leave the bigger questions to others. What I really enjoyed was force.

My applications continued, and grew in sophistication. I learned how to use sunlight to create contrast, and the moon for effect, after hours, beyond court appearances and time at the office. As such, my home was filled with evidence of my tendencies, but no one knew about them because I had walled it off from everyone.

I was a professional.

I offered professional services.

Grandpa would always correct the way I held the axe. He said that "if you do it like this" you'd be able to split it apart faster. After he needled me for a time, I'd do it his way, and sure enough, I'd split more wood.

I'd always wonder what he did out in the wood shed, since
he never let me go out there, and Grandma said little. This
made my right hand shake not being able to go out there
with him. Then, as I walked past the house I'd kick the
gravel up against the chickens, not for any particular reason
but just because I wanted to.

The way they walked in to my office; the way they
looked around with a combination of peevishness and
condescension like they weren't sure they'd stay.

It was the Rolex. It was the Tiffany bracelet.

His designer jeans were cut too tight for his age along with
the dress shirt that he'd dressed down. It was the overly
polite vernacular and the dandyish, affected handshake.

They wanted my professional services, they said, having
heard that I was scientific and discreet. They made it clear
that they had to keep up appearances, for both personal and
professional reasons even though they wanted little to do
with each other.

After I seated them in the small, private conference room
with coffee, I felt a rush of disgust coming into my mouth. I
pressed my shoe deep into the carpet so hard I thought that
I'd surely break the sole. Under the table I pulled the pen
apart and tossed it into the garbage. These people disgusted
me. They were unthinking ideologues with too much money.

They wanted me to mediate their separation in such a
way that they could maintain appearances to family and
local community while living apart—all in the same, large
house. He'd take the left wing, she the right. They just had
to build a second garage so they wouldn't have to see each
other; this would also require building another means of

ingress-egress into the property. Blah, blah. And blah, blah.

I threw my coffee out into the sink I was so disgusted. Then I went to the bathroom and slammed my cyst against the wall. I returned and took their information with a smile; wrote everything down; gave them my fee schedule; told them we could do what they wanted. Then I sent them away and spent the next twenty minutes trying to wash off their ignorant stink.

The rest of the morning I sat at my desk drawing up papers for various clients, unsettled with the small brown stain on my white shirt. It was almost unnoticeable, I was sure, to others, but it bothered me greatly. I had many shirts—so it wasn't that—but I couldn't stand imperfection. This is not to say that I had a form of obsessive compulsiveness. It was deeper, my problem, and revolved around the impossibility of attaining the ideal that was always "round the corner." It plagued me; as such, I'd be more apt to throw away the shirt, which I did later that day.

Yet, this didn't take away the distaste I had for the new clients I'd met earlier, which triggered my desire for the application of force. In the underground parking lot, I accidentally scratched my key against a couple of new cars, pissed on another, and unfortunately backed into the side of a fourth. Fortunately, for me, the video camera didn't have the angle on the area so it was not recorded. Then I sped off to the highway and then to the suburbs.

Our marriage: we were really, really good at keeping up appearances, too, and neither one of us went in for yelling and screaming. This made for a fairly quiet house even when the two kids came along. In addition, we had two cars, one for luxury, which we drove on the weekend, and the other for errands because it was better on gas.

There were her parents and my parents, the neighborhood,

our friends old and new, and school activities. It was, to be sure, a pure bourgeois existence. We had chosen paths that had well-worn grooves and easy to read sign posts, which made for an ease in living and a semblance of predictability. This is not to say that I didn't have part of the garage and an old wood shed for my personal projects. This is where I applied force, pounding and grinding to my heart's content late into the evening, keeping the company of a space heater, a light bulb, and the old refrigerator we'd originally gotten for our wedding.

I'd pound; scratch; drill; fill; clean; tighten; loosen: any way that I could apply force to objects. I'd never get my fill and even when it was past midnight, I'd come back in, climb into bed, and the restless would continue with the dreams. Black, shadowy, cutting, jagged, fragmentations that resisted discursive formation.

I'd pick my fingernails, especially at night during the dreams; pick my face on the sides; pick my toenails when I was at home or in my office. The picking made me feel calmer, and I'd try to clean it all up so no one would notice.

I'd stretch my tie out as well, actually pulling it off when my door was closed. I'd take it off and stretch it out, then I'd put it back on while pulling it to its maximum length. This made me feel good when the knot was done.

Yet, these applications were unsatisfactory. The sort of experience of power I was after was a version of Macht not Kraft. I mean to say that I wanted the brutal, pushing, hitting, unmeasured version, not the cultured, refined, moderated sort. That is, I didn't want to filter my natural tendencies through cultural proscriptions. However, this led to a real conflict for me: the bureaucratic stylization of my career in contradistinction to the purity of my natural, instinctual impulse.

My solution was to take it out on my clients, the ones I despised. This is not to say that I could accomplish this in a crass, outward way for that would ruin everything; nor did this mean that I had to revert to a clever, craftiness. What it did mean, in short, was that I'd hurt some of them and would also terminate others, knowing that it was a matter of time before the law caught up to me. This was my plan, to apply force in such a way that I'd recognize it; that they would recognize it: My need required a witness.

The irony was that in my cavalier attitude about getting caught—and this was not arrogance or hubris—I thought myself protected by some weird, distorted strain of natural justice. This made my daily professional life all the sweeter, knowing that my plan was intact and that all I had to do was execute it.

I went on like this for quite some time, as my practice grew and my marriage flourished. Occasionally, I get part of a Sunday afternoon to myself, in which I would putter around the garage, watching the old television I had placed out there, grabbing cold caffeine from the refrigerator, and playing around on the Internet. It was very much like being a teenager, hiding out from the family. But the time was short lived, and I'd be jerked back into reality by the commitments and obligations for which I'd signed up a long time. This created an urge in me to spend more time at the office, which I did on Saturdays because I could legitimize it. Sundays were harder.

Yet, I'd always go back to work on Mondays with a smile, my shirts pressed and starched, my shoes shining, and my attitude positive. Perhaps it was the pot I'd started smoking now and again that relaxed me, or the pharmaceuticals my M.D. prescribed. However, what was happening involved a subtle displacement of my direct need for force into discursive language in my head; transposition. I was now thinking about my need, putting words around it, describing it, interpreting it, but not instinctively acting it. I could send this after I used the pot or the liquor that I kept in the garage.

A couple of days after the elixir or the smoke would wear off I'd be right back to where I started. Then my need to pound or kick, or the like, would be stronger than ever—a sort of rebound effect I think it was. It would kick in and occupy my thoughts relentlessly until I fell asleep.

As the years passed, I would engage in the subtle teaching of my two boys the great pleasure of force—Macht—without suggesting anything direct or significant. However, I could see their eyes on me all the time, watching me, modeling me, noting and cataloguing my expressions, my words, and my behavior.

I was, in sum, building an army of sorts.

SIX: THE PRIEST

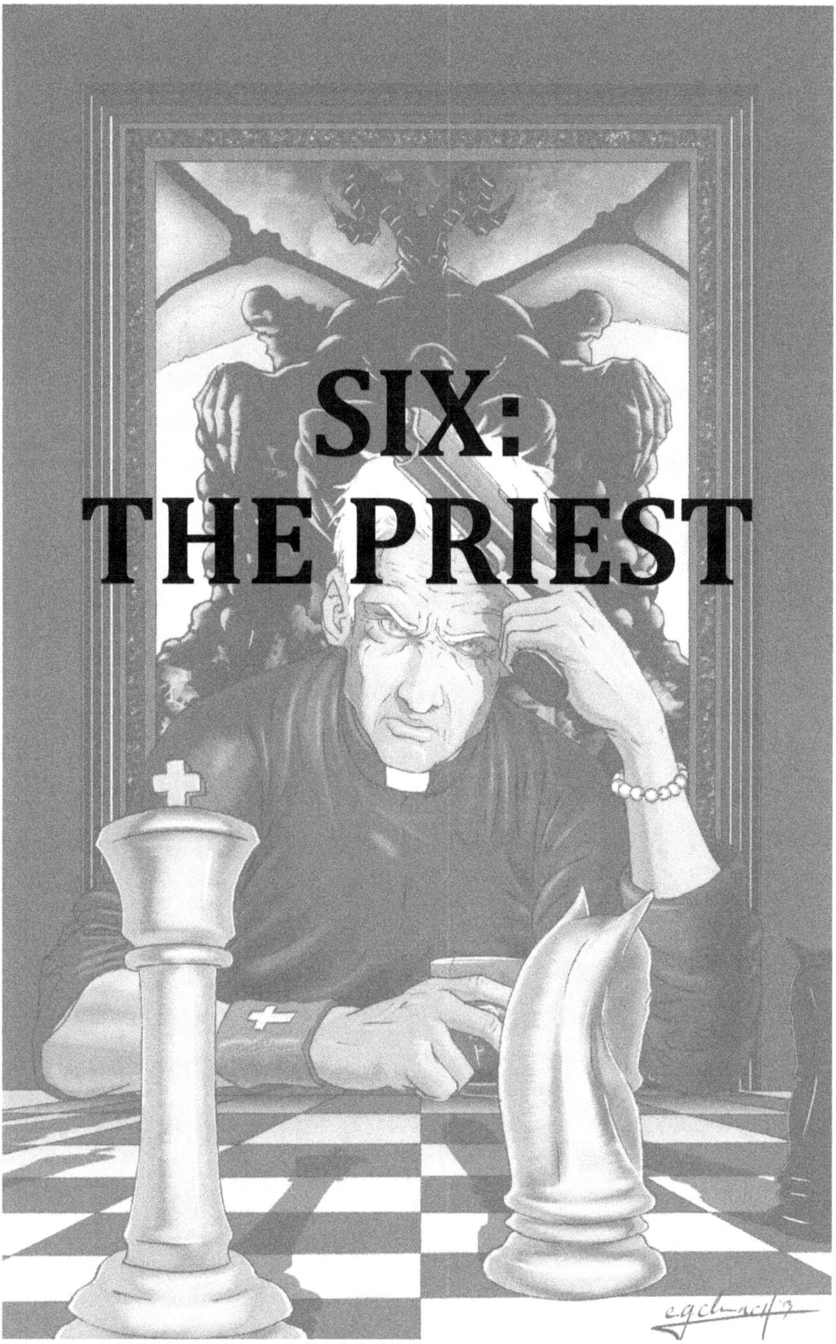

It was stuffy in here. Dark. Musty. The wood was old. I was tired. The pain in my belly was more intense than usual, and I was out of the analgesics I took for it. My headache was back but I'd fight that too with the pain relievers and some fresh air.

I wandered out of the rectory and sat down in the small dining room, which also operated as a receiving room for out of town guests. There was no one there and the emptiness of it felt heavy.

"Are you ready to take your tea," she asked, calling from the kitchen next door.

I looked around the dining room where we had entertained important guests just the night before but I felt none of their energy; it was like they had never been here and it was just a concatenation of rugs and wood and space.

Breakfast was quick, and I headed for my office downtown. I was in a heap of trouble with a number of people and the stress of it had really sapped my energy over the last few years. I hoped it would be over soon, especially given that the "hearing" was tomorrow and most of it would be resolved then.

There had been suspicions amongst the town's affluent that there was another Socrates in their midst—an uppity priest from a poor background who was trying to change the world. Through a series of clever moves, the Archbishop had become aware of his own potential risk, and therefore arranged for trial in another forum—but I knew.

I had my own "friends in high places," which is how I was warned about the commission. Unfortunately, the anger that seethed through my veins had started to ruin my health, especially because I no longer knew who was my friend.

The commission hearing was tomorrow, not in a criminal court or anything like that; nor was it in the Church per se, but there was a hearing on some very important civic matters about which I was accused of "rule-breaking." Penalties would involve the loss of my ability to engage in a number of activities and projects that I had been involved in for decades; it was an ugly matter. As it was articulated to me, I was viewed as a rogue that must be stopped, particularly because my sense of justice violated the powers that be.

I went through my normal day of activities and obligations, went back to the rectory at 3, and after a Scotch got up the nerve to call him. It had been a long time since we had talked—he was someone from the old days, and a life gone by a long time ago. There was by now a sense of urgency, which even the housekeeper noticed as she pushed a vacuum cleaner by me in the hall.

"Are you alright?" she asked.

I looked up and nodded as she continued down the dark-red carpet. Back and forth; back and forth. I sat back and sipped the Scotch, looking to the phone then back to the Scotch.

"Hello?" the voice said.

"It's me. I need something. I'm running out of time."

He didn't ask what it was all about; the substance and the detail of it were both unimportant; what was crucial was that I hadn't spoken with him for 15-16 years, before the seminary. At that time, we had to finish up some tough business that had started when we were both adolescents, which we did. I figured I might not hear from again except for a funeral or a wedding here and there.

But here I was—inviting him to have supper, which he declined—instead showing up to the darkened room with the booze later when it was quiet and all the staff had gone away.

"It's a tri-lemma," he said. I didn't respond.

I could see the shadow of the weapon in the dark yellow light. He smelled of liquor and leather; lack of hair but the eyes remained. Shallow. Hollow. Very piercing, seeing.

I remembered back to the graveyard; it had been a grave year. We had laid him to rest even though I saw him leave the park. I could hear his footsteps across the leaves as they crackled. He smiled at me but continued walking. This and other events shook my belief system in death.

"If I don't get rid of him, my career is over—-all of it. I have too much to do to lose this."

The shadow of the weapon traced images cross the wall; muffled sounds came from the far part of the rectory, a meeting or something; memories of things lost, like the girl I'd fallen in love with at 16: they almost banished me for it.

We drank two scotches and talked about the old day while we talked about the present. It was tri-lemma, with only one option authentic, two others passive. My headache mixed with the scotch, which was worse. "You have no real choice," he said.

Why did I become a member of the clergy anyway? What was I trying so hard to prove? My shit smelled too.

"What are you going to do? Want me to handle it?"

I poured him another drink and we sat in the dark yellow filled with hardwood, pictures from all over the world, and a well-worn rug. A picture of the Angel-Beast was prominent on the wall, and he pulled it down to examine it. "I received it anonymously several years ago. It's beautiful, isn't it?"

"It's bloody scary," he said.

The blood spilled out on the floor all over. I had purposely cut myself to see what it would be like and I watched the life cascade out of me. Precious time. No recipe. Precious time. Choices were no small order. This was after he died, after the crinkling of the leaves after he walked away from his own funeral. Or was this just a book that I had read? Perhaps it was a book in which I was protagonist?

I was so pissed about this situation. If I did nothing I would lose everything. If I had him do it I would lose my soul—I would still be resentful and weak. Yet if I did it myself I'd risk jail and the loss of everything. So in essence I either had to risk losing everything or accept my resentful passivity. Acting meant murder. This is not to say that I was trying to collapse the tri-lemma into a dilemma, but there was a clear distinction between the active and the passive.

He left quietly, and after a sleepless night I received news, by courier, that the hearing had been re-scheduled for two weeks out, which was good because it gave me time to consider my options.

I drew an owl sitting in a tree, but the tree was skeletal, having lost its leaves to the fall. Combining an idea I got from a book in 3rdgrade, intermixed with autumn experience just before the snow came, I had anchored inside me a semiological platform: endurance, vision, Spartan needs, fierce intelligence and self resolve. It was the best picture I ever drew, and I put it away in a chest for another day.

Someone suggested I made my career choice based on guilt, and I had come to believe that might be true. Everything I had worked for in my life was on the verge of collapsing—being annihilated—and my only way out was to violate the very principles of my life. If I didn't, I feared that it had all been for naught, and the details don't matter. What's important is that I was about to lose all; either way I went it would be a total loss in some way. A zugswang of profound dimensions.

The absolute impossibility of it all—the zero-point—became even more accentuated when I both realized the moral implications and the force of the resentment seething through my blood. I was being effectively murdered, by the complexity of political forces that had grown beyond my control, and no matter what my choice, all that I had given—the coherence and integrity of it-would soon be gone.

I put the scotch glass under the running water and set in into the sink. On my way out of the room, I turned the light out and stopped. He had left something on the chair, the weapon, so I grabbed it and headed upstairs to my room—hiding the brown paper bag under my coat. I smiled. Then I slept—a tired, restless, troubled sleep.

By 5 a.m. I was up for good: angry, and full of a rage that I had been harboring through booze, church doctrine, and habit. I bumped into the bathroom door and cut myself shaving. Breakfast coffee seemed bitter and watery.

"Did you see the front page?" she asked. "The city council has okayed the waterfront development—a lot of people will be kicked out of their houses; won't be able to afford them."

"Sonofabitch."

The fuckers had moved in and ruined everything: their clothes on the lines and the wrecked cars in the yard. Then the city cleaned it up by tearing everything down. The bourgeois moved in.

Speech acts: Saying something to cause a consequence. Moral statements were a version of this. "Good" meant approbation and "Bad" or "Evil" meant disapprobation.

The morning was hell. I got my headache back. Blood swimming to my temples. Not listening to most of what the department secretary said to me, or to my students. Instead of staying on campus for lunch I headed back to the rectory and viewed the weapon.

Speech acts.

Then I fell asleep to the blood in my temples.

There was a rash of calls for the next few days, advice about what I should do. Sleepless nights and the bitter interpretation of coffee ruled me. I was beside myself with rage—I broke dishes, a pencil, accidentally threw away a draft of an essay I had been writing.

From what I heard there was a witness who was going to testify against me. The charges had been filed, and if they found against me, the life I had developed over 40 years would be over.

After a few discreet phone calls, I received an anonymous note at the rear door of the rectory. It was someone I'd had a falling out with several years ago. He'd lost a job because of it, and had since kept a file on me, waiting for his chance.

I knew him.

I spent the rest of the week going about my obligations and chores, and then over the weekend, a week before the re-scheduled hearing. I looked at the weapon but always put it back in the crinkled bag, and deep in a box filled with papers in the closet.

"Father, it's so nice to see you."

We sat in the office together and looked at the dusty, stained pictures on the wall, ghosts from a former life. I wondered what would happen to the books when I passed.

[In another life: she put the pictures and knick-knacks into boxes, the few remaining that had been left after the service. The children didn't want any of it and the "personals" meant nothing anymore. As such they would end up in a store that sold junk like this, or perhaps in the junk heap itself.]

I could feel the end coming, which seemed all too soon even though it had been presaged for the last decade and even though I knew it would happen eventually. I had too much left to do, which seemed unfair and tragic. Now this motherfucker was going to destroy what little I had left— unless.

So in a quick series of decisions and attitudes, I resolved to use the weapon. I had his address and a gun with a silencer, no serial number, which would be untraceable. So I kept my equanimity and went about my business. I hid the rage, like I saw so many others do. But I was seething. I had been wondering in the last few years of my life if all the ideology I had bought into was all a lie.

My back hurt. I picked up a cardio-vascular infection. My superiors were irritated with me; they knew of the upcoming hearing and were probably relieved that someone else was going to have me removed.

After a Friday event at the Church, I slept the next day, all day, and then made a choice.

We sat in the barn on top of hay bales in the warm summer chewing on twigs and discussing the better part of frolic. Looking back through the wistful mist of time and lost memory, I wished for the warm blue sky that wrapped its arms around that barn.

With the future unknown, we played, and imagined ourselves in various ways, but still landed in the blue of the sky and the warmth of the yellow-sun. I'd sit in my office later—much later—which was only in the past few years, and reminisce alone about some of those ephemeral times. The gossamer of my youth, I guess. Still, the smell of the green pasture lingered, and her red hair would be permanently etched in my memory.

I left a letter in my desk drawer that would direct the housekeeper and custodian to collect my office effects and send them to the library.

I could sit and explain my resentment but I didn't want to; even afterwards when the cops came I had little to say. It was far more than self-protection; it was more than revenge. It was full-on, explosive, rage though contained within my analytic, methodical method.

Even the way I expressed the rage was contained.

~

I found him in the dark and I shot twice. Two muffled pings ended his life while people who lived in the rectory thought I was in my room, having shared dinner and a drink in the sitting room. I was back soon enough and no one ever knew, but this wasn't the point; nor was morality the point.

What was the point was that I had taken control over my life instead of cow-towing to the ideologies that had taught me such control. I was a good student!

~

The hearing was cancelled. Shortly thereafter, within a year, I retired. My resentment wasn't yet sated, so even I spent my time—going forward—with new community-based projects, tying up loose ends, and using the silencer. You see, now I was like a junkyard dog who'd killed a chicken. I loved the taste of blood.

Thus begun a new phase of my life, and I started letting go of the ideals and moral proscriptions I had spent most of my adulthood developing. Such foolishness!

I developed a new relationship to the dark, and my health problems receded.

No one ever knew. What was also most pleasing was that I quickly overcame my guilt: the beauty of the kill was just too satisfying.

SEVEN: THE FAST FOOD WORKER

Employee
of the
Month

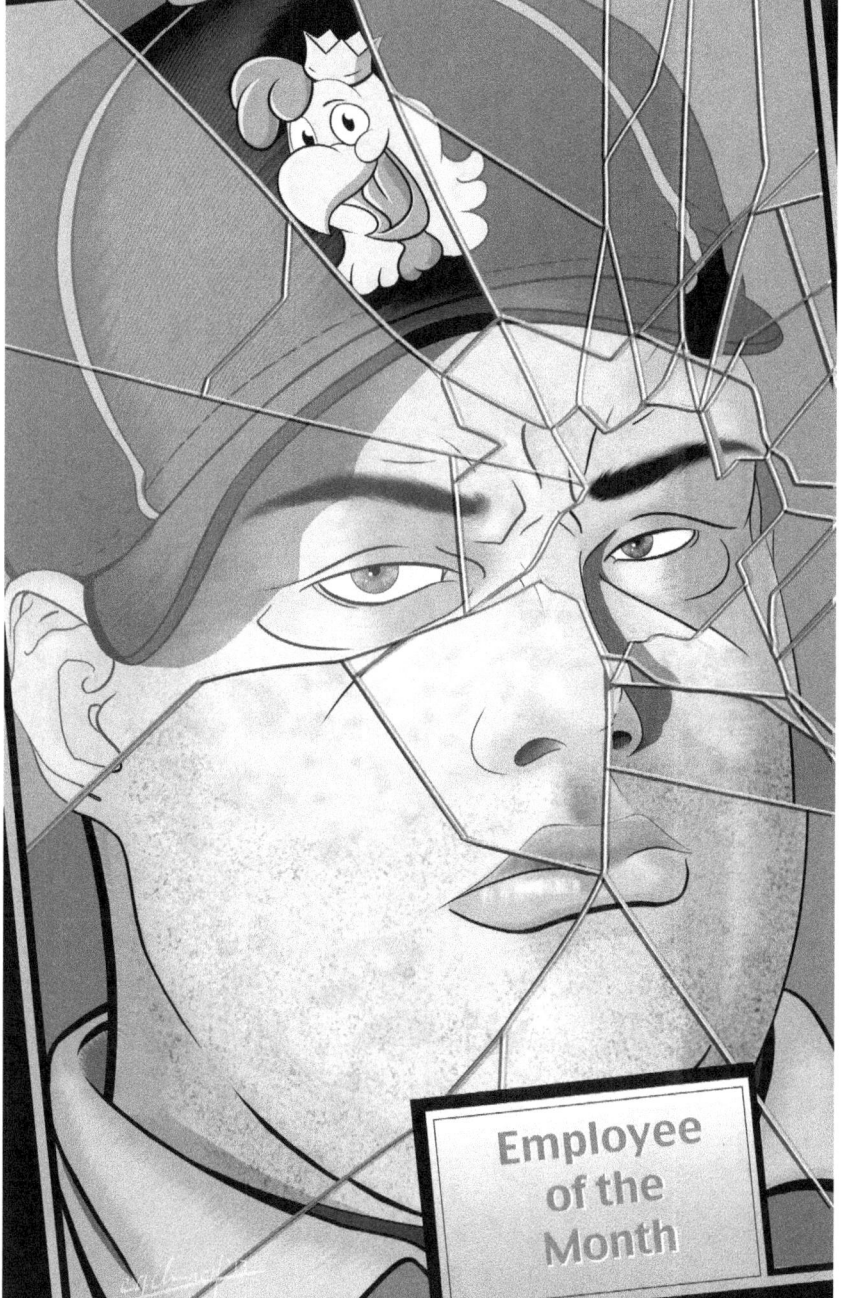

Employee
of the
Month

Someone thought that they had recognized him from the newspaper photograph. He—the person recognized—was overweight. His face was red from blisters and pimples and his eyes were guarded like a hawk's.

Whenever he would serve me, he'd always do it perfectly like a surgeon, but in his quick, perfect movements there was a vitriol that felt dangerous.

It was every month or so at first, then I got so busy at work that my fast food behavior ramped up to three times a week, so I got a chance to interact with him more often. We developed a relationship: I'd try to be friendly and he tried not to be. His speech and movements were perfect, completely in line with job expectations and protocols. This way he was sure not to lose his job.

I tried to engage him in a human sort of conversation from time to time but he'd have nothing of it. He would dig in and play his part with even more alacrity.

He'd always seem more at ease with himself the day after the newspaper reported another kill. At first, I didn't put the two together naturally—-it was only in retrospect—-but eventually I started correlating as we all do. At these times, I'd drive up, make the order, and pull into the 2nd window. They'd only use the 1st window when it was really busy then one worker would take the money and the other give out the bag. But when I went it was slow, so there'd only be the 2nd window in use, and he would always be there.

"How's your day?" I'd ask. In exchange, he'd only speak in terms of the fast food business at hand by asking a question about sauce or something like that. And it didn't matter which variation I would use: I'd get nothing out of him. On the other hand, he'd always proffer comments on his own about the shitty weather or something underhanded that referred to his work situation, or to politics, or _____ [whatever]. It was always something, but as I reflect on it the substance of what he said was less important than the way he would articulate it.

Then a curious thing happened. On occasion when work was slow I would muse about him, just think about the penetrating stare, the excoriating delivery, or the just-plain-bad nature of his attitude. He was negativity personified. It came on slowly at first, but within a season I discovered that I thought about him almost every day. I chalked it up to intrigue or curiosity so I could justify the time, but I had gone through the whole menu more than once and started to know the nuances of the place. I became a fast food expert, and this netted me subtle advice on what had the best ingredients, or whether a special was coming.

His acerbic tongue got worse, and it seemed that the friendlier I became the greater were his vituperations. They seemed calculated not only to ward me away to the outskirts of the web, but to advise me of danger. On this point I had no real proof, but the fact that my palms were sweaty and my blood racing after I picked up my order were enough. If I had known better I would have either not gone around him anymore or just not thought about it, but this was not the case. I was fascinated and seduced, and thoroughly interested in this guy's story.

The newspaper accounts were heinous and gruesome:

someone had been raping women and then cutting them up into little pieces after several hours worth of torture. And when I'd read these accounts, I'd think of him, wondering if he were at work or what he was doing. I felt the same sweaty palms and would become hungry.

I'd sit and re-read the stories, albeit with the most important details removed. I admit that I wanted to know more; I wanted to know the precise ways that he would inflict pain and taunt his victims until they couldn't take it anymore—until they would give in and he would terminate them. I wanted to know what happened. What was so hard for me, and I would nervously look around as I shuffled the paper at a public restaurant or wherever while I thought these thoughts, was that I wanted to be there.

I thought myself sick and repulsive for having this prurient interest but I couldn't help myself. As such, one day as I wheeled in there and ordered from the value menu, I asked for the complimentary paper and pointed out something inane about all the killings. I said something about wanting to watch. His reply indicated a lack of interest but I thought I saw his pupils dilate and then retract quickly so as not to be found out. He mumbled something about voyeurism, smiled sardonically—though wryly—and excised me so he could deal with the next.

My food was always the same just like my life. It was a usual palette of foodstuffs, schedule, people, values, and ideas. Even though I had been brought up to believe in freedom of expression I was starting to realize that the sort of world that I lived in had greatly constrained this notion and that perhaps I was more like a thing than not.

This always led to behaviors like going for fast food. I might add that try as I might I could never actually see the name on his nametag. There was either food or black felt markings on the whiteness of it, and he'd always manage to turn at such an angle that I'd never get it anyway. I did, however, think that I heard someone call him Charles or Booth or something like that; I guess it didn't matter.

My own life, which I was becoming aware of with greater perspicacity, was a cul-de-sac. I had finally become aware of the numbed out condition into which I had been bred, that I had developed in a sophisticated way, and about which I was so tired. The vicious nature of the food worker had triggered my awareness of my condition—of myself. Now I felt it like day-old breathe, acidic and disgusting.

This led to poor work performance which I justified through my adopted filter—the worker—developing my own brand of bad breath to accompany my attitude. As I continued with my fast food habit, I too gained weight. I could see it in the mirror and feel it in the tightness of my shirts. Red marks started popping out on my face and I felt sweaty all the time. And still I'd go for fast food.

He'd started handing me the complimentary paper without my asking but only on the days that it reported another killing. I think it was his way of satisfying my need for experience without saying so, and without my being there. Yet, I felt like a relationship had been established, and I respectfully waited for the next cue.

Over the next several weeks nothing happened, then months without moment, and still I waited and still I came around. For a while, it seemed like he had disengaged with me, which caused me great disappointment. It agitated me to no end because I thought we'd established some sort of relationship. It may not have been a friendship, but it seemed a matter of courtesy that our ongoing exchange would continue.

I started pressing him a bit, making all sorts of insinuations but he wouldn't bite, knowing full well how frustrated

I was becoming. I thought I could even detect a bit of salacious glee in it for him, knowing how much I liked reading the sorts, how much I enjoyed our short exchanges [even though they only amounted to a few seconds each transaction they meant the world to me].

I did notice that on occasion, my food wasn't as hot or as fresh as it used to be, and sometimes I'd just throw it our without saying anything. I felt rejected, even abandoned, by his change in behavior but I continued coming around hoping that he would re-engage with me.

After several months, I could see that his attitude was becoming even more difficult for him. He had lost the complex and graceful way that he'd trash his society, and it'd come out like a bad batch of fries. He seemed to hardly notice me—we'd gone back to me having to ask for the paper—but at least there was an interaction, and for that I was grateful.

Then, just after the holidays, and the cold sniping winter, and the advent of spring, I came around again and again for about two weeks and he wasn't there. Eventually, I got one of the others to let me know that he was out sick, or that it was his mother who was sick—one or the other—for which I was greatly disappointed. I would have liked knowing but I bore the frustration in silence, having my own problems at work and at home, and concentrated on them until he returned.

It was one unexpected but hopeful day, and I drove up and heard his voice over the scratchy, hard to understand speaker system. I was instantly filled with such satisfaction; such joy. This time I ordered a full meal.

Even though his face still sported the red acne blisters; even though his hands and wrists were still puffy; even though he didn't give me much notice; there was a new confidence about him that coincided with a new rash of killings that had happened over the past two weeks. There were four in all—young women—who had been violated sadistically before being murdered. This time, however, he offered the complimentary paper to me without my asking.

This made me consider that he had rejoined our alliance and that everything was back to normal. Over the next several weeks, as well, even though he was sarcastic and acerbic in his comments, some of what he said was ostensible speculation about where the next might occur: the railroad tracks that shot across the south side of town; one of the two river basins where the water trickled out into the flood plain; the dirty part of town with all the alleys; one of the country roads; the industrial area with acres of mostly unused, gray buildings. I got my clues, which excited me to no end.

With the regular meals and clues, I pursued my life with new zeal and intensity, exploring the Netherlands of my hometown, following the riddles. I gained new relationships, awards at work, and started spending time at the bookstore reading serial killer novels. It was a back and forth between fast food lunch and the bookstore, when I wasn't working.

I learned that my high school girlfriend was back in town, and I did the very best to avoid her: My life was already fulfilling, and became more so when I found one of the bodies from a recent kill. After he found out, the friendliness that I thought we had developed soon ended; he later left for another job, and I was left to my own devices.

EIGHT: THE PORN SHOP BOOTH CLEANER

I met him in group therapy—long-term, insight-oriented, mixed gender, adult. His name was Mack or Larry, or something like that: real American sounding. He had no money, was living off of state funds and some account that his grandmother had set up for him when he was young.

He had not cultivated anything for himself. He had no education. He barely knew how to read. His social circle was limited to an on-and-off girlfriend with whom he fought and occasionally slept. He had no colleagues or family; no community at all except for the group, which he continuously tried to stay in for free.

The financial part of it thus became a contention because he figured the therapist owed him the service without payment. At first he agreed to pay the fee; then it became a reduced fee; then we all talked about it; then he walked out mad; then we agreed to pay for him; then we talked about our feelings about paying; then he quit showing regularly and when he did he was disheveled; tired; angry.

From then on—the anger and resentment of the group—his attitude changed from hopeful to an alienated resentment. He saw himself an outsider. He stated "we were treating him like he had always been treated and was, therefore, considering a departure from the group."

Like clockwork, the group therapist encouraged that we all

talk about it, but then the guy, Mack, threatened to leave. I think that the therapist knew once he left he'd never return so he strongly—and perhaps—too much so—requested that he stay.

He did. We talked about his life: the girl he slept with had no job and no teeth. His family was dead. He'd been kicked out of the police academy and from then on had drifted, sponging money, working odd jobs, all this until he got older and realized that life had passed him by. By now, he was pushing sixty, his face gaunt, his former sinewy muscles gone—turned mostly to bone and skin, and we were the only people he had left. Except for the Porn Shop Booth.

We let him speak at length, and later the session ran over— which was rare and which never happened again—and we discovered his world. Perhaps it was his way of staging the exit, I don't know, but we learned about his life in such a way that we all felt ashamed.

He worked in a porn shop and had been for over a year. At first it was to fill in for the missed shifts of others, then part-time, and now it was full time. He literally spent 40 hours per week in a porn shop booth. This amounted to him watching the cash register, making sure that no one stole magazines or movies—and cleaning the booths.

He reported it with reticence: walking around with the squirt bottle of ammonia and other cleaning agents, the smells of the booths mixed with the ammonia. There was cigarette butt end-smoke, sweat from labored breathing, a nasty, indefinable smell from the hypodermic syringe refuse—plastic, brown or white powder residue, blood. There was excrement, piss, and semen. It was basically a toilet and he was the toilet-man, the cleaner of the abjectivity of the porn shop. 40 hours per week at minimum wage. This was just enough to pay for a crappy room with a hot plate, budget groceries, bus fare, bathroom supplies, movies with the woman—and group.

It was a bizarre scenario he recounted, the porn store lighting a muffled, smoky yellow, the patrons furtive, wearing upturned collars & caps—all subtle ways of taking back what they had chosen. He could smell booze and cigarettes on most of them, and the stench of black tar heroin or the white powders of a few substances would waft through the air every time a door opened.

He, himself, did not drink anymore because he couldn't afford it but he smoked like a chimney, having to sneak out to the back alley when no one was in the store. He'd prop the door open, he said, and puff away until someone came in or someone left one of the porn booths.

He'd wear gloves when he cleaned, the white-yellow ones they sell at the medical supply stores. Part of it was easy, mopping the main floor, then the individual floors of each booth. Sweeping the entrance and the outer sidewalk was a piece of cake, so he did this part first, and then again.

The hardest part he left to a function of disgust and dread. This included the porn booths that were frequented by businessmen, bikers, construction workers, husbands, boyfriends—almost everyone who wasn't afraid to be seen, but this was why most of them wore hats or upturned collars. On the other hand, they all realized that they were all in the same boat, which created a tacit cooperative by which they'd pretend not to notice each other and most certainly would say nothing ever upon fear of self-implication.

This left the booths. This was where the absolute abject bottom of our humanity resided. Drug use, homosexual and auto-sexual behavior, alcohol were rampant. Even beyond that, one could apprehend the alienation and isolation of the patrons—many of them—finding respite and solace out on the edge of town in a strip mall where no one would know.

The group member said that he would overhear some of them talking to each other from time to time, commiserating their shitty worker lives, marriages, and holidays. I could hear in all this a closure of their stories, a yielding to the socio-political forces that forced them from a tender age into super-ideologies of normatized behavior. Needless to say they were all highly angry, resentful, and by now numb. This brought them to the porn shop.

He recounted stories of gay sex, straight sex, and narcotic use. He talked about one guy who would come in for hours—just once a week—but he'd bring a wad of twenties, which would each feed the booth for one hour.

There were two movies going at all times in each booth. That way you could watch one movie while investigating the others by fast-forwarding to the best of it.

There were others who didn't sit in the booths, and were there to buy toys; others were there for quick pickups in the seedy parking lot, or they'd go somewhere else, sometimes to a nearby car wash at night when it was dark.

But it was the booths, he said, that carried all the vermin. Blood. Semen. Sweat. Needles. Bottles. Cigarette packs. It was the absolute garbage pit of everything that was wrong with our society. What really pissed him off was that he had tried for years to carry an honest job, do an honest day's work for a fair wage, but unfortunately none of them paid enough to live on. The current job was just another in a long string of frustrations.

For several weeks, he made careful insinuations about "having a story" to tell, and needing reassurance about confidentiality. If you'd been a fly on the wall you could tell that the group thought he was engaging in hyperbole. At some point he felt the issue was cleared so he started in one day—he hadn't brought any money for the fee—but he started in nonetheless.

A guy had come in one night browsing around the store, making under the breath comments about a "piece of shit." Finally, Larry realized the guy was referring to him—the swaggering, drunk, prick with the new boots was calling him a piece of shit. This was on the heels of being reprimanded by his boss for not getting things right, so his adrenalin was up and the blood pumping anger deeper and deeper into his marrow.

I could go on about what the guy looked like, but it didn't matter. What was at stake was the last vestige of dignity this guy, Larry, had. He recounted that the guy "accidentally" dropped some magazines on the ground and when Larry went to pick them up the guy cursed at him.

There was no one in the store and only one person in one of the booths, busy listening, busy seeing. Larry engaged the smartass, questioning about his attitude in a diffident sort of way. This exacerbated the situation, and because the guy was drunk, he escalated the epithets as they pirouetted toward the cash register, toward the back door.

That's when Larry pulled out a pipe he kept behind the counter. He took it out fast, hitting the man with all his rage. He hit him in the temple and the man went down. It was only a brief second that Larry looked down at him, horrified at what he had done. But this second passed quickly as he summoned all his strength—he was thin and not too strong—to drag the man out into the alley.

He was terrified about what he had just done, his hands shaking, but he had enough resolve stored for the past fifty to carry out the act. As he explained, there was nothing for him to do but pull the guy into the alley and kill him, which he did. He hit him on the head three times more and then stuffed him under some boxes and Styrofoam in the large blue bin. There was a bit of blood but nothing that couldn't be handled with the squirt bottle and a rag.

He was scared to re-enter the shop from the back door, halfway expecting the police to be there, but nothing was amiss. You could hear the porn coming from the end booth, and in a few minutes a man and a woman entered to look around. Other than that, there was nothing. In the three minutes before the front door opened, he was able to clean up in the bathroom. Everything else was in the alley garbage can.

The couple bought a few toys, then he went to the bathroom and finished cleaning up. He made the rounds with the mop bucket, a smile on his face as he thoroughly cleaned the store. He pulled the surveillance tape, destroyed it, and tossed it into the garbage, too but only after he was certain it was completely cut up and ripped to shreds. Then he spent the next several hours of his shift eating his lunch, selling toys, organizing magazine racks, and generally feeling good about himself.

Everyone in the group was stunned. Even though most of us had seen a lot of things in the world, we'd never been exposed to something like this. We glanced at each other, watching the time clock, and prompted by the therapist, shared feelings. I think we were all stunned, but eventually someone asked if the story were actually true. Someone else said he was in shock. A few of the pragmatic and moral members asked if he'd gone to the police. Then the session was over and the therapist thanked him for sharing.

On the way out the door, Larry spoke with a newly found confidence in his voice and a slight spring to his step. "There's more," he said as he left.

The next several weeks were filled with anxiety, fear, judgment, and discussion about what should be done. After all, someone had been murdered. However, it got worse—far worse—because Larry also confessed that after the trash had been taken to the dump, a lonely place on the outskirts of town with no monitoring and a lot of hungry birds, he felt his confidence being restored. In fact, he could not remember ever feeling so good, so powerful, and so in control of his life and over his destiny.

Some of the group wanted to call the police; others, a lawyer. The therapist reminded everyone of his duty of confidentiality—this was part of the deal from the beginning. He proffered that we should "bring our feelings and thoughts to group." After all this was why we were here: to understand ourselves better, heal, and perhaps help each other.

However, the content of Larry's behavior seemed to go beyond the pale; it had unsettled the overarching worldviews of all of us and had unseated the very reason we were meeting. My God, he had murdered someone. To make matters worse, after the first few weeks of reactions, he mentioned again that there was more.

No one had suspected him of the killing, so in essence he had thus far gotten away with it. But it was much more than that. For him, in contrast, it was his first real taste of freedom, which he could not articulate but could only enjoy. He said that he finally "felt alive," and that even just the memory of it provided him a profound joy and pleasure that he could experience over and over. He said, "All things seemed possible now."

This event overshadowed all others, and it came out that group was disintegrating. Everyone else's story paled in comparison to Larry's, and so even when everyone was sharing there was still the dinosaur in the room. To further the farce, Larry continued to share about his experience cleaning up the refuse in the porn shop. This included detailed stories about the fluids they left in the booths, and in one case it was excrement. Someone had literally left a pile of human feces on the seat in the front of the booth.

Then he started recounting a second killing, and a third, but he did it with such equanimity, sharing his private joy in such a way that you felt like family. It was like letting your immediate family in on a job promotion during dinnertime, but the effect was horrific: two members left the day he started sharing about the additional acts, never to return, and others would show up late and cancel without notice.

It was apparent that the group was fragmented—more so it was annihilated—and for this the therapist had to acknowledge it. Membership had gone from 10 or 11 down to 7 or 8, but attendance had become irregular so it was a shifting group. Larry made a couple of off-handed comments about quitting his job and moving on, but no one seemed to notice. New dramas had sprung up, and we took on new members. A few others quit, and Larry's bill accumulated. He said that he had other things to share, but he was largely ignored except in passing.

I overhead a couple of our members in the hall quietly musing about the possibility that Larry had fabricated the whole story, details and all. Then I quit, and moved on with my own life. Several months later I ran into him on the street and gave him a ride. He had found new work, he said, and was leaving the state, heading up north. He said he had always liked me because I listened to his story without judgment. Then I dropped him at the corner and never saw him again. That was 40 years ago.

NINE:
THE BOY
MADAME

He'd been little as a boy and was always the last one picked at the baseball games. By the time he was twelve, he found greater pleasure in playing with girl things, enjoying girl games, than he ever did being with boys.

He was thin—not a twig—but of slight build, and always wore his hair long from the time his mom cut it that way in first grade. Being picked on didn't seem to bother him. He had a friendly face, and was able to get out of conflict by not buying into it.

He had one of those first names where you could go from boy to girl by changing the last letter; it was therefore, easy to go back. As such, he was able to switch his name when he went to a progressive out of state college. He joined the gay students club because there weren't provisions for transsexuals. He later figured out he wasn't homosexually inclined.

He had suffered greatly. His macho Dad was ashamed. His mother, though gentle, was dismissive in a subtle way. Friends and family took sides, dividing like the parallel wakes from a boat—connected but divided. School institutionalized his struggle, and getting older reinforced his oscillating consciousness—the competing forces of his inner nature and the pressures of the outer world.

He'd been raped before, both as a boy and then as a

girl. Because of this s/he was wary, and had developed somewhat of a strident and sarcastic tongue with which she warded danger away. She was not to be messed with.

Her hands were noticeable, too, with fingers a bit longer than you'd expect and feet a man's size; but it was the fingers I'd notice because she would clutch them as she spoke—clutch and release, clutch and release. I felt the warning.

I was one of the customers—a regular—so I saw things. A couple of thugs beat her up once and took protection money. On the phone I could tell she was in battle with someone: one of her girls had been murdered over a turf war. Then the cops came and pushed her around one day. It went on like this for a while.

They called her "Madame," but I learned that her name was Gabrielle. She'd been on the phone—it sounded personal, like she was speaking to a sister or an old friend, and because she didn't hear me coming down the carpeted hall, she allowed herself a few tears.

She quickly subdued her emotions, straightened up and smoothed her dress, then greeted and dismissed me in one quick motion: She was the Madame, was all business, and too care of things with a stiff upper lip.

When she showed up a few weeks later, bruised and beaten, a small cut on her cheek from a knife, those of us in the lobby exchanged subtle glances, but then went on our way. That was the code: mind your own business and say nothing.

I was a nothing: A fat, wealthy, and a sorry excuse for anything. My wife worked all the time and my kids were preoccupied with video games and any other image that moved. I had not cultivated anything for myself save for money, a belly, and properties. My golf game was nothing special, and I had figured out that because I was inconsequential my only recourse would be acquisition.

A few years ago, I'd seen an advertisement for a call girl service, which I eventually used. She was young, like my wife used to be, and the experience was not altogether unpleasant. For many months I went underground, then one day heard about a place where I could go to unwind. It was a cash deal, and one time led to another, and another. Much like a neighborhood bar or a family bowling alley, this became a second home for me. Nothing else in my (w) life motivated me, which ended up in my regular visits here. They had a bar, and the company was straightforward: my new home.

Yet there was ugliness here in the subdued lighting, the furtive glances: the cash and the lipstick, the skirts and the perfume. It was prurient and unsavory. It excited aggression in me, the sort that one wouldn't talk about in polite company or even with one's friends; the sort of aggression that you read about or see in the movies; the sort of aggression that always triggered violence. This is what I had started to feel around that place, toward that Madame.

I had a complicated admixture of feelings toward her. On the one hand, she had completely transformed into a woman, and took the time necessary to make herself attractive. Her mathematical ratios were nearly perfect, her lips, hips, breasts, calves all in order. She had an uncanny way of eyeing everyone in the room with her highly refined peripheral vision. I always took this to mean that she was vigilant because she had been knocked around in the past.

On the other hand, she disgusted me. The reconstructed Adam's apple, the long fingers, the feet: from the back, and if the light was just right, you could tell that her shoulders were on the larger side. Added to this was the neck scarring from the electrolysis, the eyebrows, and so on. But it was more than just these individual features. There was a pale, sadistic sickness about her that infected the room whenever she walked into it. It was a mangy, doglike countenance that led to imaginations of putrifying flesh, poor smells, and cheap fingernail polish.

This was the nefarious side of abjection, implying a negative dialectics that would presence the worst in us—-the ugly, un-golden, decaying, darkness that seduced us into the nether side of consciousness. This was the ambivalent form of consciousness of alienation, both being and not being at the very same time. It was a combination of these thoughts along with the yellow light and the way she'd perfected her role. This, of course, triggered what little understanding I had of the ontological difference—and my freedom.

I considered myself un-free except in fantasy, the manifestations of which I enjoyed here at this safe, dirty, fallow place. She, the Madame, was like a dead crow lying on pavement, bright red blood un-coagulated and still warm. Legs up in the air, eyes missing. It was as if they had been plucked out. Myself, I was the perfect gawker, couldn't do anything myself except to follow corporate logic and bourgeois ideas. Her red lipstick was the blood mixing with the dirt of the pavement—the filth of the society from which all travelers here wished to escape. She was a dirty band-aid.

Home was worse: more abject in the darker sense; filthier, dispensing perhaps even more alienation via the blank stares and the processed foods. My children busy learning the ways of the new world order; my spouse involved with someone else—we were only together in order to avoid the stress of separating our monies. The situation as a whole was gross and putrifying, like the decaying flesh of the Madame's spirit.

It went like this for months, spending every bit of cash

money I had in order to spend time in the yellow light
of it all, watching her lipstick lips move in accord with a
routinized arabesque that drew us back to her brothel week
after week. Thus, it was no wonder that I imagined killing
the vermin in there; cutting at it until I could separate it
from the good part; providing the antidote for the poison
in her. It was not surprising that I bought a knife from the
pawnshop.

I then started enacting my fantasy. I'd look at the bright,
thick blade, which I sharpened. I cut myself once with it
to see it work. Then I put it in the car under the seat "for
protection" if anyone asked. But it was not for that; rather,
it was an essential element in my reflective process, a
sign of my expression. It was a symbol for my disgust and
resentment.

~~~

The following year from a modest hotel in the South I read
a small story about a transsexual Madame who had been
viciously murdered. The head had almost been severed
from the neck.

The brothel closed and everyone was under suspicion.
When my wife and kids found out they disowned me, so I
was divorced and unmoored. When the police interviewed
me, they concluded that I couldn't have done it—for reasons
I never understood.

I had taken cash money out of her till, which got me south
until I got into my accounts. To this day, there was no
mention of theft; everyone was more interested in the
savage pool of blood that they found in one of the rooms.
Over fifty times, she had been cut; over and over until
nothing was left but blood and putrifying flesh (it had
happened on a Sunday when few people were there. By the
time the cops got there, it was a decaying, stinking mess.).

Some years later there was an additional inquest about the murder. Stories of the Madame hit the papers. Continued investigation led to a former corporate employee who had frequented the place. Then it led to a southern town that had its own serial killer: vicious rapes and stabbings, all of victims.

By then, I had moved on and since I had used an alias, felt little anxiety. In my new home, with my new wife and her children, I enjoyed many years of marital bliss, church activities, and a renewed interest in my health. I decided not to ever frequent places of ill repute, opting instead for a life of peace and domestic reveries. The fact that I never heard from my former wife or children comforted me greatly. It was the ease of it all that I enjoyed.

TEN:
THE
LIBRARIAN

I finished my third cup in the break room and headed to my station in the reference area. It was not quite 8 a.m. so I was nearly alone, and sat quickly reading the local newspaper.

I'd been here through all the changes, stemming back to the card catalogue era, and the lack of air conditioning. Pictures in my locker proved the passage of time, which had left me in a grizzled and compromised position.

I'd been passed over several times for higher level supervisory positions which, ostensibly, was due to my lack of social skills—it was thought that I was a bit autistic and perhaps sociopathic, though no one would openly admit to any of this when confronted about it. Instead, I had become one of the library workhorses; as such, my fate was to work long hours, making sure that the tedious and monotonous was finished.

I had not married nor was I gay. I was just alone, living a solitary life as a solitary person in a solitary job. My friends were books except for when I'd head home to the rooming house. I'd have to walk past Apartment 101, which was occupied by the old lady who managed the place. She was okay with me—I'd been here for years—but there was always the latent threat that if I didn't pay the rent on time she'd not cut me any slack. Thus, my relationship with her was alienated by our contractual arrangement, much like my library post.

My family was dead except for a brother and a sister who I hadn't seen in years—every now and then I got a postcard or a Christmas wish but beyond that there was nothing. I did not belong to any groups, clubs, or organizations; there was no bar or activity that involved others. I just worked, although on weekend mornings I'd sit outdoors at a café, drinking coffee, reading, looking at people peripherally.

Younger employees at the library would go through a set of phases with me. At first, they'd be friendly, regarding me as someone senior who could help them. Then they'd realize my one-down position and would join the subtle condescension. I'd pretend not to notice and would thereby join them in this derivative conspiracy. However, years of isolation and pejorative dynamics created a "bad taste in my mouth," a distaste with which I had learned to live, though I could feel the sickness tightening its grip on my life and my soul.

I received the usual raises and concessions, and everything went from season to season, year to year, my spirit waning, vitriol increasing. I had started to lose weight a few years ago, due to lack of eating. My abstemiousness was less physical and more mental, I think, in retrospect, because I felt that I did not deserve anything other than what I had, which was loneliness and alienation. Interestingly enough, all the comforts of home were not enough to overcome the bad taste in my mouth or the way I was made to feel: "my place in society." It seemed that everyone was just waiting to get rid of me; they were patient in their rejections.

The couple of years I tried church didn't work out well for me either. When the postcards stopped and I wan invited to fewer work lunches, I realized how much I was just hanging on a thin branch of life. Every time the wind would blow, I'd end up in the stark cold, waking in the middle of the night to the howls of all the monsters and demons that I was sure were out to annihilate me. And so it went: from the angry, fearful nighttime to the shamed, condescended daytime. As such, I was on edge of rage—a former irritation and annoyance that had became a solid anger.

I intentionally suppressed my anger by becoming more polite, resolving that I was a better man than everyone else around me. In fact, I engaged in complex machinations in my own mind, "giving" my shame back to those who would shame me. Yet, how could I also give away my anger—that solid pounding that pushed against my temples everyday? This was my query.

It seemed that I was at the end of my useful life, certainly to the border of my existential trajectory. There seemed to be nothing I could do: the plot was set, and I but a player in it. This closure frightened me, mostly because I had never dealt with this situation, one in which my possibilities had shrunk to a zero-point. My freedom could, therefore, only come from fantasy, which I engaged in regularly, most of it centered in rage and resentment. These complex stories were all future oriented, which balanced out the power of my memory, pulling me into the past.

I hated the growing bureaucracy: forms and processes for everything, so much so that work became a series of tasks that would manage them. Real human interaction was structured around the structure. As such, there was an infinite reservoir of human experience that never percolated into presence. This cauldron included my anger becoming-rage, which led to sleepless nights, weight loss, a nervous tick in my face, and white knuckles. I knew my job so well that I successfully covered these marks of anxiety, and when I'd leave at the end of the day, I'd grip the steering wheel so hard that my hands would hurt long after I made it home.

It was a Janus head, the anger, operating both for me (as instructing power) and against me (as creating resentment). This had created a division within the core of my soul that both created and sustained me, but which was also destroying the inner fiber of my self. I made sure that I completed all of my job tasks perfectly. In fact, I obsessed so much about this perfection that it became the goal of my behavior—the perfection, its impeccability—and had little to do with the specific tasks themselves.

Thus, the quest for this perfection became the foundation and reason for my life, though it was unstable and stressful. It resulted in a red hue to my face, pulsing veins in my forehead, the white in my knuckles, and a general shortness of breath. My interpretation of temporality changed. I no longer had command of the dispersion between past, present, and future—everything was future. This driving forward did not leave me any respite in the moment, so you can see how the architecture of my very self was starting to erode, crack, and lose containment. I was becoming ephemeral—not just an unessential repository of shame—but an unimportant voice that had been instrumental to the very creation of the library, of all the voices.

My tasks got harder, and there were more of them. This meant that there were more chances for perfection, and more chances to escape shame, with the side effects. One of my colleagues in particular—two of them actually—seemed to be a constant impetus for my displeasure and misery, so I resolved to end it carefully, with precision and perfection.

She was a stick and he had red marks on his face from eating too much candy. She smoked and drank coffee; he played video games. Together, they instigated subtle and invidious forms of sadism at my expense. The details are unimportant, frankly, but they involved all the usual ways one could sabotage a co-worker. This led to daily fantasies about their savage demise.

I had nothing left to pursue except perfection: in the routines of my personal life and in the obligations of my occupation. I was a librarian!

I had read more books than most but one often just tore the other without any kind of genuine reciprocity: not the kind of world I wanted to live in—reverie of negative dialectics. And so it was, living this tension between the white knuckles and the ontological wholeness I perceived in my quest for completion-perfection-compliance.

I did start spending more time in the recesses of the library reading about the sorts of violent tendencies you may have that you don't want others to know about. I felt like my life was over, and in fact wanted to end it. I wanted to take away, by my own hand, my situation, ending it for all time. And so I fantasized—

Yet, I was unsatisfied by this conclusion. This was the resentment operating in me, a counter-force that wouldn't allow me to detach. The truth is that I'd saved enough money so that I could leave even though in that case I wouldn't receive my full retirement. This scratched uncomfortably against my obsession with ontological perfection, which allowed me the fuel to continue against my own freedom. I could clearly see how resentment and the quest for ontological wholeness could prevent one from acting in one's best interest. This was happening in my case, but I felt powerless against my own "power."

I continued working, hunting down my salvation, an acrid and bitter taste in my mouth, as the days passed focusing more and more on the abjective elements in my life. They were all becoming venomous, an insidious drive that accentuated the poison in my soul, and I didn't know a way back to my virtue. I was lost in the spit, the blood in my temples, the stench of fear and rage, the precision of my murderous, violent tendencies.

And yet, all this competed for homeostasis and respite—an end to my original position: I was in a bad spot, had been for some time, and could not see a way out.

The glint of the blade mesmerized me in the morning light.

The destructive forces of nature no longer hurt me.

The pulling sensation of strangulation captivated me in my dreams.

I took a few days off and drove to the coast. I drove back and nothing had changed. My co-workers had boundless energy for sarcasm and cynical sadism, I imagine, because of their own torturous pasts. So what? I had no empathy for this or for them. I just wanted them gone, yet it was curious to note that vanishing would not have been enough.

Instead, I desired their suffering—their shame, then torture. By having them join me in this way, we could enjoy it together, this false sense of meaning, this disjointed alienation that drove us against one another, against ourselves. I admit that I was taking great pleasures in this imaginary revenge—but it was an ambivalent revenge because half of the energy was still focused on my own pain and death.

The glint of the knife in the afternoon sun; the abjectivity of death I found on the sidewalk, little carcasses of former life that had been swept into the concrete jungle we so loved. And my knuckles whitened. And I enjoyed pressures of all kinds, the pushing of it coincided with my need to integrate everything—the bain of post-modernity.

Weeks and months passed, and my new supervisor wrote up a complaint against me. He was 30 years younger than me, more educated, and better dressed. This pushed me deeper into that underground place from which I had been born, and which I sought my whole life. I now relished violence, and pursued it in films and imaginations, books and fantasies. I bought the gear. I made a plan. I pursued perfection with even more exacting detail, logging the contours and aspects of my moods throughout the days, recording the peccadilloes, slights, and sins against me with exactness.

It was going to be suicide or murder. All other options were closed to me, my life past that point when new roads can be built. It was the time when our facticities seemed to outstrip our transcendence, unless we considered drastic and serious measures that involved ontological violence. These were the self-induced behaviors that seemed to "fight back" against the ruptures that would occur naturally.

I slept less. My hands started shaking. Although I continued in my assiduousness, the fluidity between moments become disjointed and divergent, a staccato like connection that faltered and spit last vestiges of life. I thought about the North Country and the wolves, Hayes Creek, Milena, the priest and my friend the bookkeeper. I still dream about the island with the laborers, my predilections for fast food and my time in the porn shop doing research on perverted libido. I had read all the books on thanatology and morality, and little had developed into understanding. Then I made my decision about what I was going to do about my situation. I had finally learned the art of engagement, at least discursively. I would soon employ it for my own ends— my soul.

Homo Homini Lupus

Heart-of-Fire

Heart-of-Fire is an imprint of EPIS Press dedicated solely to fiction, poetry, and other literary production that is related to psychoanalysis, phenomenology, and Critical Theory/ deconstruction.

EPIS Press
31 Fort Missoula Road
Suite 4
Missoula, MT 59804
epispublishing1@gmail.com
www.episworldwide.com
www.episjournal.com
www.episeducation.com

also from Kevin Boileau

When they found his corpse, there was blood, vomit, and shit. It smelled like piss in the alley underneath the metro-line where the crows were when the sun came up Sunday morning. He was "in rigor," they said to the reporters before they took him to the Medical Examiner's office. One of the police officers found his identification, raising his eyebrows as he gave it to his older partner. "Yeah, it's him..."

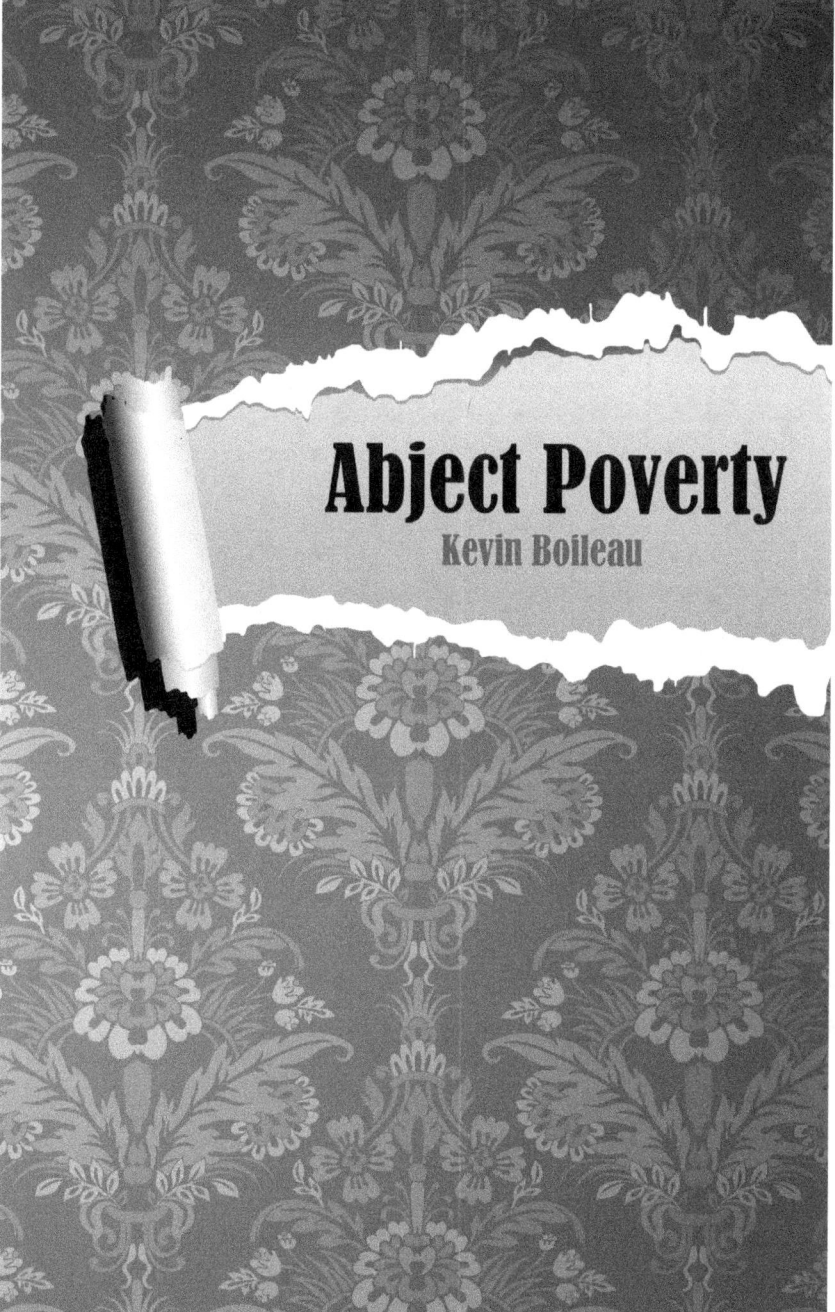

Abject Poverty
Kevin Boileau